PENGUIN CLASSIC CRIME

VERY COLD FOR MAY

William P. McGivern was the author of several novels,
including *Night of the Juggler* and *Soldiers of '44*. He
died in 1985.

VERY COLD
FOR MAY

By William P. McGivern

PENGUIN BOOKS

PENGUIN BOOKS
Viking Penguin Inc., 40 West 23rd Street,
New York, New York 10010, U.S.A.
Penguin Books Ltd, Harmondsworth,
Middlesex, England
Penguin Books Australia Ltd, Ringwood,
Victoria, Australia
Penguin Books Canada Limited, 2801 John Street,
Markham, Ontario, Canada L3R 1B4
Penguin Books (N.Z.) Ltd, 182–190 Wairau Road,
Auckland 10, New Zealand

First published in the United States of America by
Dodd, Mead & Company, 1950
Published in Penguin Books 1987

The characters, places, incidents and situations in this book are
imaginary and have no relation to any person, place
or actual happening.

LIBRARY OF CONGRESS CATALOGING IN PUBLICATION DATA
McGivern, William P.
Very cold for May.
(Penguin classic crime)
Originally published: New York: Dodd, Mead, 1950.
I. Title.   II. Series.
PS3525.A236V4   1987   813'.54   86-22519
ISBN 0 14 00.9368 0

Printed in the United States of America by
R. R. Donnelley & Sons Company, Harrisonburg, Virginia
Set in Caledonia

VERY COLD FOR MAY

CHAPTER ONE

J AKE HARRISON picked up his hat and coat from the cloakroom attendant and was walking across the lobby of the Saxon Club when he heard his name called. He turned as a blue-uniformed page hurried to his side.

"Call for you, Mr. Harrison. A Mr. Noble."

Jake hesitated and in that fraction of time a good deal of his amiability departed. Finally, he said, "Okay, thanks," and went over to the bank of phones beside the elevator.

Before lifting the receiver he checked through the events of the day in an attempt to guess what Noble wanted him for; but the day had been without incident, neither more nor less frantic than usual.

Shrugging, he lifted the phone and told the club operator he was on the line. She asked him to wait a moment and he heard a click as the connection was made. Then Gary Noble's voice blasted into his ear.

"Jake? How soon can you get down to the office?"

"Oh, hell," Jake said.

"Jake, I wouldn't bother you if it wasn't important."

"Oh, sure. Look, I've an eight o'clock date with Sheila at Dave's. What's up?"

"I'm sorry about lousing up your plans," Noble said, with somewhat too much solicitude. "But listen; Riordan, Dan Riordan, called a while ago and wants to see me tonight. He wants us to handle his public relations. You know this is the biggest damn thing that ever happened to me, Jake. Riordan owns mills, mines, factories—"

"Yes, I know," Jake said. Noble's enthusiasm was working insidiously, and he began, almost against his will, to fish up the things he knew about Dan Riordan.

War Contractor. Genius of Production. Free Enterprise. Know-How. Money. Married after first wife's death. To entertainer, show girl, something like that. Son in Air Force. Good war record.

"What's his trouble?" he asked.

"Well, we didn't go into the details, but the Hampstead Committee wants a look at his books. You know what that usually means."

"He'll need a lot of help, then."

"You've got to get over here," Noble said.

Outside Jake could see light, picturesque snow falling on Michigan Boulevard and the hazy street lamps lent a pleasant, Dickensian flavor to the scene. He sighed.

"Okay. I can make it in fifteen or twenty minutes."

"One other thing, Jake." Noble sounded both cautious and puzzled. "He mentioned May. May Laval. Said something about her being in a spot to hurt him. Asked me if I knew her, and so forth."

Jake said, "That fits in with the rumors, doesn't it?"

"You mean about that book she's planning—the exposé on high living during the war?"

"Sounds logical," Jake said. "I'll get over as quickly as I can."

He hung up, then called another number. A moment later a quiet voice said, "Dave's Radio Bar. Dave speaking."

"Dave, this is Jake. I'd like you to do me a favor. Sheila and I planned to meet at your place at eight. But I'm tied up now and—"

"You want me to tell her you'll be along soon?"

Jake smiled. "I couldn't have put it more neatly myself."

"Well, I'll tell her, but this kind of stuff is why she left you in the first place. She's nobody to push around like a call girl."

"You're right, Dave," Jake said. "But take care of her, will you?"

He put the phone down and shrugged. That was the best he could do for the moment. Sheila would probably understand.

Waiting at the curb in the light snow while the doorman signalled a cruising cab, Jake thought about the news he'd got from Gary Noble and a small frown touched his face. He was a slender, gracefully built man in his late thirties, with graying hair and lean features that were saved from austerity by a normal expression of good humor.

But he wasn't looking particularly good-humored as he climbed into the cab and gave directions to the driver. He was thinking of what Noble had told him about May Laval. Except for that, the Riordan account would be a routine chore.

But the element of May in the equation made everything else unstable.

The cab made a U-turn in Michigan Boulevard and headed north toward the Executives' Building. Jake lit a cigarette and glanced out at the dark bulk of Lake Michigan and the traffic that formed a chain of light along its shore.

He had known May Laval quite a few years. Ten, at least, he thought. She was about his own age, thirty-eight. The facts about May were not too mysterious. She had come from California to Chicago as a girl of nineteen, a very beautiful girl with golden hair and large candid eyes that had surveyed everything in the city with delighted astonishment.

She had gotten into a few shows on the merits of her beauty, which was real and fresh, and after her third show closed, had surprised quite a few people by marrying its backer, an elderly meat packer. The marriage hadn't lasted long, and May had come out of it on the way to being a wealthy woman. She had proved then that there was something behind her big blue eyes, by investing her money shrewdly in South Side real estate that doubled in value within a few years. Jake had met her about that time, which was shortly after her second marriage to an orchestra leader had turned out badly. He had liked her, and they became firm but casual friends.

May's talent as news copy always astounded Jake, who was doing features for the *Express* at the time. She had a flair, or rather a passion, for weird and dizzy escapades. Her antics could range from a nude and nocturnal bathing party in Chicago's Buckingham Fountain, to the successful bidding for a Poe first edition that every bibliophile in the country had wanted. May had color.

She became known over those years as a character's character. Her plushy Victorian home on Astor Street was crowded with politicians, judges, gamblers, newspapermen and, for variety, there might be a handful of derelicts picked up personally by her from West Side soup lines. May knew everybody; everybody knew May.

During the war she reached her zenith as a colorful personality. She was unofficial hostess to the important men who came to Chicago to buy and sell properties in seven figures, a Girl Friday to the men fighting the war of priorities, allocations, contracts, and logistics.

It was said that a meeting of the Allied Chiefs of Staff might have been held in her parlor on a dozen different occasions. It was said she knew the tastes in women of every general in the army above the rank of brigadier. And it was said she had made a killing in the market with tips from contractors and brokers, who exchanged this information in return for the right word in the right ear at the right time.

The end of the war seemed to bring May's era of curious importance to a close. The press was slightly weary of her, and there was competition from returning G I's, from strikes, readjustment, and the other agonies of peace. The days passed when May's name could be found in three or four columns in every edition of every paper in town.

Jake realized that he had hardly seen May since the end of the war. She had made a few sporadic attempts to recapture the attention that had always been part of her life, and then she'd gone to Sun Valley.

That had been all, until the rumor of her book began to float around. According to the vague but prurient reports, the book would be one to end all books on the war. It was to be an exposé, based on her diaries, with names, dates and telephone numbers, of chicanery and fornication on the highest of levels.

It was to be Madame Récamier telling all in four-letter words.

Jake tossed his cigarette out the cab window. He couldn't help but be amused with May's latest brain storm, even though it was likely to embarrass their prospective client, Dan Riordan.

Jake liked May. He knew that the stories about her, both the good and bad, were exaggerated wildly.

Those who didn't like May said she was a vulgar exhibitionist, a spoiled and ruthless creature, who had to be pampered and spot-lighted every minute of the day. Friends of hers, and they were many, said she was a generous, amusing woman, quick to help anyone who was down, and dangerous only to stuffed shirts, bullies, and prudes.

The truth lay somewhere in the middle, Jake guessed. May was a good deal of a phony, but amusingly so. Her chatter about art and literature, her first editions and signed paintings, were all cultivated with a frank eye to their publicity value, and her demand for attention, while not always charming, was hardly ruthless.

On the other hand, she had a sharp sense of humor, and her flair for sarcasm was usually reserved for people who deserved it.

The truth was that May was born to be looked at, to be admired, to be discussed and speculated about, and unless all this was happening at the same time,

May was apt to be miserable.

Jake gave up his reflections as the cab drew to a stop before the Executives' Building. He had no idea what May's interference might mean to the Riordan account. But it was a safe guess that from now on things would be exciting.

Jake stepped from the elevator at the thirty-fourth floor and walked briskly toward the solid glass portals which bore the inscription: Gary Noble and Associates, Public Relations.

The reception room was dark but, upon entering the long, panelled hallway that led past the art and fashion departments, Jake could see light coming through the half-open door of Noble's office, at the end of the corridor. There were voices and laughter coming from the inside and, also, the aroma of Noble's twenty-eight-year-old Scotch.

Jake walked down the dark hallway and, after rapping on the half-open door, stepped into Noble's office. He saw two men and a woman with drinks in their hands, and Gary Noble, who was working behind the bottle-cluttered bar that was normally hidden by a sliding section of the mahogany panelled walls.

"Well, there you are," Noble said heartily. Gary Noble was not impressive physically, but his energy and enthusiasm were as overwhelming as a tidal wave. He was short, bulky, and fiftyish, with effectively disarranged white hair, and eyes that were startlingly blue against his darkly tanned skin. Gripping Jake's arm, he pulled him toward the center of the office. "Jake," he said, "I want you to meet the Riordans."

The tall, powerfully built man standing at Noble's desk, Jake recognized as Dan Riordan, clubman, industrialist and tycoon. Now Riordan looked tired and anxious; his thick black hair needed combing and his hard, strangely pale face was lined with worry. Standing together at the windows were a slender brunette of perhaps thirty-five, and a sandy-haired young man in a dinner jacket. They had been studying the world globe which, for some reason, Noble considered necessary to his office.

"Our senior account executive, Jake Harrison," Noble said.

Riordan shook Jake's hand with a quick, powerful grip, and smiled briefly. He seemed to be controlling his nerves, or his patience, with difficulty.

Noble led Jake to the couple at the window and made the introductions with a nice deference to the lady, who was Denise, Mrs. Riordan. The young man was Riordan's son, Brian.

Denise Riordan murmured something and smiled at Jake. She was attractive in a smooth, polished fashion, and nearing forty, but her deeply tanned skin and slim figure made her appear younger. Underneath her excellently styled black faille suit, her body had the relaxed suppleness of a dancer, and her bare legs were evenly tanned and beautifully shaped.

Brian Riordan was tall, thin, with sandy hair and light gray eyes. He wore his dinner jacket with grace and was in the process of getting thoroughly drunk.

He beamed at Jake good-naturedly. "Now, I suppose we'll have to get down to business. Probably means the drinking is over."

"Not on your life," Noble said, with a bellow of Rotarian cheer. "Let me fix that glass of yours. There are some things more important than business, damn it."

Jake knew that not even the sight of his mother lying under the wheels of a truck would slow Noble down on the way to a lucrative business appointment; but Noble had the gift of infusing his banalities with a desperate conviction that made people unconscious of their pointlessness.

Dan Riordan cleared his throat, and said, "I think we'd better talk about business, Noble." He added drily, "I hate to spoil the party, but I'm rushed for time."

"Right," Noble said. "Let's pitch right in."

Jake lit a cigarette to cover his smile.

Denise Riordan walked to the brown leather sofa that extended along one wall and sat down, crossing her legs. Brian took a seat in a chair on the other side of the room and yawned comfortably.

"City air gets me," he said, to no one in particular.

Noble was refilling glasses, so Jake said, "You don't live in town then?"

"No. I live in Wisconsin, at Dad's lodge. I come into Chicago once every week or so to get sociably drunk."

Denise glanced at Riordan, who was leaning against Noble's desk, and frowning at the floor, obviously not listening to the conversation. "When do I get to see the lodge?" she asked him, smiling. "I've seen the patio in Palm Springs and the hut in the Everglades, but no lodge."

Riordan glanced at her, and his face cleared as he smiled. "It's not a very exciting place. Perhaps Brian will have us up some weekend if you're curious."

"Delighted," Brian said.

Noble distributed the filled glasses, then pulled the leather chair from his desk and pushed it over to Riordan; but Riordan shook his head.

"I can talk better standing," he said. He took a sip from his drink, then faced Noble, his feet spread wide apart and his shoulders squared.

"Here it is," he said. "Last week the manager of my Washington office called me, and told me that the Hampstead Committee had come across some deals of ours that they wanted explained. Two days later they sent a preliminary investigating team to Chicago headed by a fellow named Gregory Prior. Prior is in town now, and has sealed my books and is getting

11

ready to go through them with a fine tooth comb. When he completes that end of the investigation he'll report to Washington and, if they think they have a case against me, I'll be called before the committee for a hearing."

Noble had been nodding sympathetically. He said, "The government has a mania for investigating people. However, what's Prior likely to find when he looks into your books?"

"He'll find I cut corners," Riordan said. "Hell, the Nazis and the Japs were cutting corners, weren't they?" He tapped a thick blunt forefinger into the palm of his hand. "Here was the situation I faced: I had a contract to make barrels for the U.S. Army, and our boys needed those barrels bad. This was the winter of 1944, remember. Rundstedt had driven a wedge between our troops in the Ardennes, and the whole damn First Army was ready to crack. Goebbels was shouting that they'd have Antwerp by Christmas, Paris by the first of the year. Things were bad. I couldn't beg or borrow the quality of steel that was specified in my contract, so I went ahead and made barrels with a cheaper grade of steel. I made the barrels, by God, and they were a damn sight better than no barrels at all."

Riordan stopped talking, took a cigar wrapped in tin foil from his vest pocket and began to unwrap it quickly. There were patches of angry color in his cheeks, and he was breathing harder.

Brian Riordan opened his eyes and smiled at his father. "You've got an interesting point there," he said. "I wonder if some G I who got blown up with one of those barrels would agree with you that they were better than none at all?"

Riordan turned on his son with a bull-like twist of his shoulders. "There is no proof my barrels blew up," he said, in a hard, precise voice.

"Well, somebody's did," Brian said, yawning.

Riordan took a handkerchief from his pocket and dabbed at his forehead. "Yes, there were cases of premature detonation, and of barrels cracking after heavy use. They happened in Ordnance testing grounds, too, under ideal circumstances, and with guns made to exact specifications. But that isn't the point. I made barrels when they were needed overseas, and the only crime I committed was in violating the letter of a government contract, which was stupid and unreasonable in the first place."

"Hear, hear," Brian murmured.

Riordan ignored him and continued talking. "Now, Noble, I don't want to be pilloried in the newspapers by this damned committee. Senator Hampstead is an ignorant, suspicious hillbilly who hates the thought that any man in the world has an extra pair of shoes or a second dime in his pocket. He's a sour neurotic who thinks he's God Almighty. I want you to get my story across to the papers, and see that they treat me right. Can you do that?"

"Well," Noble said, expansively. "I don't see any difficulty so far. You acted in a sensible manner, and it shouldn't be too hard to get that fact over to the public. However, I do think we should have a few more facts at our disposal."

"All right," Riordan said. "I'm no good at details, but I'll send my executive secretary, Avery Meed, over tomorrow morning with all the dope on the deals the government is worrying about. That okay?"

Brian Riordan got languidly to his feet and walked toward the door yawning. "I'm going to run along, I think," he said. He opened the door, a smile on his face. "I sympathize with you two gentlemen, you know," he said. "You've got a tough job. You're supposed to put my father's wartime activities in a rosy light. Well, maybe I can help you." He paused and glanced at his father. "The old man, in a sentence, is a liar, a thief, and a murderer."

"Brian!" Riordan snapped. "I want no more of that talk," he said, but underneath the hard surface of his voice Jake sensed a note of defeat; and he had the feeling that this was not the first time that Riordan and his son had been through this thing.

Brian seemed undisturbed by his father's reaction. He said to Noble, "He's sensitive, too. You'll have to handle him carefully." With a mock salute at his father, he walked out of the room.

Riordan jammed both hands in the side pocket of his coat and was staring at the rug with a bitter frown on his face. Denise came quickly to his side. She said gently, "Don't you worry about him, Danny Boy. You know he's been upset since the war."

"Brian had a hard time in the war," Riordan said, a defensive tone in his voice. "He—he's not to be blamed for his attitude. He had a tough time, and now he's having trouble settling down."

"That's childish," Denise said. "He had it tough, but so did a million other guys."

Riordan said slowly, "I don't think it's fair of us to criticize him for not behaving as we'd like him to. Now, let's get back to our work."

There was a knock on the door and Dean Niccolo, the agency's top copy writer, walked in. He nodded to Noble, and said, "Sorry if I'm late, Gary."

"Not at all," Noble said, obviously relieved by the interruption. He introduced Niccolo to Riordan and his wife. "I asked Dean to come in tonight after you called, Mr. Riordan. He'll be working on the copy we turn out for you, so I wanted him briefed from the start."

Dean Niccolo nodded to the Riordans and smiled at Jake. "Funny thing," he said, getting out cigarettes. "I met a young crackpot getting on the elevator." Niccolo laughed, failing to notice Noble's desperately signalling eyes. "He was carrying quite a load. He saluted me, said, '4-F, I presume,' and staggered into the elevator."

Riordan made an impatient gesture with his hand. "That young idiot, Mr. Niccolo, was my son. Don't bother saying you're sorry. He's drunk tonight and acting like a damn fool. Now, we've had enough interruptions. Noble, I'd like some details on what you can do for me before I sign the contract."

Niccolo sat down and winked quickly at Jake, as Noble began talking. He was a large young man, with broad shoulders and blunt strong hands. His hair was black and thick, worn in a trim crew cut. There was intelligence in his dark features, and stubborn strength in his solid jaw. Jake realized that he wasn't at all affected by what most people would consider an embarrassing situation.

Noble was saying, "Naturally, we can't give you a detailed program as yet, Mr. Riordan, but when we know the facts you can rest assured . . ."

"I can't rest assured until I know what you're going to do," Riordan said, with a touch of temper. "Can't you give me an idea in plain words? I like things put out clearly where I can examine them without using a dictionary."

Noble flashed a distress signal at Jake and said, "Jake, perhaps you can give Mr. Riordan a fill-in on our plans."

"Okay," Jake said. He had been studying Riordan and he guessed the man could stand honesty. "Frankly, I don't know what the hell we can do for you, because I don't have any facts. After we talk with your man, Meed, tomorrow, we may know enough to make plans. There's nothing mysterious about public relations. The techniques of the business are fundamental, but each account requires a specific application of those techniques. Part of your problem, of course, is Senator Hampstead. He's remorseless, ruthless, full of joyless reform ideas, but the country is in back of him, after the job he's done on five per centers, contract jockeys, and some of the other termites that did business during the war. His committee has standing and character. And the fact that he's teeing off on you may look bad at first. That's why I repeat, we need all the facts before we attempt to set up a program."

Riordan nodded reluctantly, and said, "All right. But I'll want a report by tomorrow night, after you've talked to Meed. And there's one other thing. I asked you about May Laval, Noble. She's writing a book, I'm told. There's a chance she may drag me into it. Right now with this damn investigation pending, she can do a lot of harm."

"Are you sure she's using you in the book?" Jake said.

"No, I'm not. That's what I'm expecting you to find

out, for one thing."

Jake nodded and thought a moment. Then he said, "I know her fairly well, Riordan. I'll talk to her and see what's on her mind."

"This May Laval intrigues me," Denise said coolly. "She seems to have you men upset. What sort of a person is she?"

Riordan ran a hand through his black hair, then shook his head. "Hell, it's not that easy. She can be wonderful. And she can be a bitch. I knew her during the war. She helped me a lot, entertaining army and navy brass, government inspectors, and so forth. You know how it was. Most of the men working for the government then were a lot of tomcatting incompetents who were having a big time away from their wives. They wanted fun, excitement and to be treated like big shots. May was great at that. And she was cheerful and fun to be with, until she'd get burned up about something and she'd let loose at anyone in sight." Riordan shook his head and smiled slightly. Jake watched Denise and saw the tightness that came to her mouth.

"There was one time I remember especially," Riordan said.

"You can save it for your next stag," Denise said sweetly.

Riordan looked at her, then cleared his throat. "Well, it's beside the point, anyway. You'll see her then, Jake?"

"Sure. It's probably nothing to worry about."

Riordan studied Jake thoughtfully. Then he said, "Remember this, Harrison. I worry about everything. I don't take chances on things turning out all right. I make damn sure they do. Do you understand what I mean?"

"I worry from ten till five, myself," Jake said, easily. "But I see what you mean."

"Okay, then let's not assume that May is harmless. If she's intending to take a crack at me, I'll make damn sure she changes her mind."

Riordan nodded good night then and Noble escorted him and Denise to the elevator. Jake made himself a drink and grinned at Niccolo. "You can take your foot out of your mouth now," he said.

"How the hell was I to know the damned idiot was Riordan's son?" Niccolo said, good-naturedly.

Noble came back and glared at Niccolo. "You might have ruined everything," he said.

"Oh, hell," Jake said.

"Maybe it doesn't matter," Noble said. "The old man took it pretty well. Let's forget it and get down to work. Any ideas, Jake?"

"We don't have anything to go on yet," Jake said. "I'll get on it tomorrow. Now I'm going to try to find Sheila."

"What do you think about May?" Noble asked, as

Jake went to the door.

"Hard to say," Jake shrugged. "I want to talk with her first. However, I'd make a guess and say she's liable to work herself into a nasty corner if she goes ahead with her book."

He waved goodbye to Niccolo and walked down to the elevators.

CHAPTER TWO

FROM the Executives' Building Jake crossed the boulevard to Dave's Radio Bar. Inside it was warm, noisy, and crowded, but there was no sign of Sheila.

Dave came to meet him, a disapproving frown on his face. "She left for home about an hour ago," he said.

"Did she seem annoyed?"

"Oh, no," Dave said. "She liked sitting here alone and being wolfed at by a lot of characters."

"Okay, I'm a cad," Jake said, and walked back to the phone booth. He dropped a nickel, intending to call her but then he changed his mind and dialled another number. The voice that answered was intimate in a brash, challenging manner.

"May?" Jake said. "This is Jake."

May was having a party, as Jake had already guessed from the sounds in the background. She insisted he come over immediately. Jake promised to be there in half an hour.

Leaving Dave's, he took a cab to the near North Side apartment where Sheila had moved after their separation. He rang her bell and when the buzzer sounded went up the stairs.

Sheila met him on the landing. He had a good view of her slim legs as he ascended the last flight; but he noticed that one smartly shod foot was tapping significantly.

"This is no time to be unreasonable and female," he said. "Noble caught me before I got away from the Club."

"You say 'Noble' as if he and God were interchangeable ideas," Sheila said drily. "But come in."

Jake put his hat and coat on the back of a chair and joined her on the low couch before the fireplace. Sheila had managed to make the place reflect something of her own personality. There were fresh flowers in a squat copper vase on the coffee table, and the shelves flanking the fireplace were lined with well-used books. Several vivid modern paintings with comparatively non-frightening subject matter brightened the flat gray walls.

"Do you want a drink?" Sheila said.

Jake raised his eyebrows. "Your tone lacks cordiality. You're not pouting, I hope."

Sheila smiled. "I don't feel cordial, but I'm not pouting. Whiskey and soda okay?"

"Fine."

Sheila made two drinks in the kitchen and brought them to the coffee table. There was an unconscious grace in her movements that Jake enjoyed watching. She was slim, with dark hair which she wore in a page-boy, and gray, candid eyes. She had an easy elegance in her manner, and good humored intelligence in her features.

She sat down and tucked her feet under her, while Jake sipped his drink and relaxed.

"What was on Noble's mind?" she said.

"A new account. Dan Riordan, the wheel, is in trouble. You know about him, I suppose. Anyway, he obviously made some bad gun barrels and is going to need a break in the papers. The government is looking into his contracts."

Sheila lit a cigarette. "And you're handling the account. Does that make you feel warm and cozy inside?"

"It doesn't make me feel anything in particular," Jake said. "Lawyers defend criminals, don't they? We're merely defending Riordan from an unfavorable treatment in the press."

"The analogy stinks."

"So it does," Jake grinned. "But let's talk about something serious. We still have a date, and there's plenty of time. How about going to Dave's and drinking some raw, green bar whiskey?"

"All right. Let's get out before Noble whistles for

you again."

Jake got into his coat while Sheila went into the bedroom to freshen her make-up; and when she came out Jake saw that her mood had changed, that her temporary annoyance had vanished. She had struck a pose and said, "Let's be gay and mad. Mad!"

Jake smiled pensively. "Why you left me I'll never know. We always had fun, didn't we?"

"Yes, but you drank too much," Sheila said. "Also you pulled too many deals like tonight."

"That's ridiculous," Jake said irritably.

"Not at all," Sheila smiled. "I wanted to be a wife, but you wanted a drinking companion."

"Good God," Jake said. "You sound like some creature who's just been dragged to civilization from darkest suburbia."

"Also, I never got adjusted to your working for a fraud like Gary Noble," Sheila said.

"Dear, you're beginning to rave. You work for Gary too, remember."

"I handle an honest account, the only one he's got, I could add."

Jake shook his head as he followed her down the stairs. "I may be insensitive, but what the hell is so wrong with Gary? He's a public relations man, and he's a fathead, and he has a dull, acquisitive attitude about money, but outside of that he's not too bad."

"Well, let's not quibble about it," Sheila said. "You

asked me why I wanted a divorce and I told you."

Outside they walked the half block to Lake Shore Drive to catch a Loop-bound cab. The air was cleanly cold and a sharp breeze was coming off the lake.

Sheila moved close to him and hugged his arm. "I'm in the mood for Dave's," she said. "It's a perfect night for a warm, mellow bar."

"Oh, damn," Jake said, and tried to sound surprised. "I just remembered. We've got to make a stop. You know May Laval?"

"I've avoided her at a few parties." She let go his arm. "You just remembered, eh?"

Jake waved to a cab. "Word of honor, this won't take a minute."

They climbed into the cab and he gave the driver May's address. He turned to Sheila but she was gazing with pointed absorption at the lake.

"Now is this an adult reaction?" Jake demanded.

"What's so wonderful about adult reactions? We had a date, remember?" She looked at him coldly. "First you stand me up for Gary Noble, and now you're dragging me to May Laval's bordello like a piece of baggage. What sort of reaction, adult or otherwise, do you expect?"

"Do you think I enjoy this sort of thing?" Jake demanded.

"Of course you do. That's one of the reasons our marriage never grew into a rose-covered institution.

25

What do you have to see May Laval about?"

"May knew Riordan during the war. She kept a diary during that time which she now intends to make into a book. Riordan is afraid she's going to tee off on him and that, plus a Senatorial investigation, is just too much of a bad thing."

"This is getting lovelier by the minute," Sheila said.

"You don't like May, do you?"

"That's not the point. I like being treated like a partner in the evening's plans, instead of a gate crasher. And I don't like May."

"Oh, come off it," Jake said. "May's only trouble is that she's too adjusted. She's living exactly as all you chaste and conventional harpies would like to live, so you treat her like a leper."

"Don't be so frantic about it," Sheila said. "Can't I dislike her for more interesting reasons, such as, for instance, that she's a man-hungry, pampered, over-dressed bitch?"

Jake grinned at her. "Charitable, aren't you?"

Their cab stopped before a two-story brownstone house in the old-fashioned but eminently respectable Astor Street neighborhood. Climbing out, Jake saw lights shining through the drawn curtains of the wide bay windows, and heard loud, excellent jazz coming from the first floor.

"Just a few of the girls in for a sewing bee," Sheila said drily, as they went up the steps.

The wide, polished door was opened by a maid in a frilly black and white uniform, who led them through a dim foyer to the arched entrance of the long, elegant parlor.

The room was decorated in a rococo modern Victorian manner, with oval mirrors in chalk-white frames hanging against the flat green walls, and white china lamps with fat roses shining palely in the design. Underneath the bay windows at the end of the room was a great curved divan, covered tightly in green striped satin, and before it, a vase of roses rested on a low coffee table. Orderly clusters of small oil paintings were hung about the room, slightly below eye level, and the great, ornately carved white fireplace was flanked by bookcases that reached from the beige carpeting to the high ceiling.

There were perhaps thirty people in the room, and their high-pitched conversation and laughter mingled quite well with the jazz that poured from the black lacquered player. The women present were slim and expensive-looking, and the men were precisely the sort who could afford them.

Jake noticed a couple of municipal judges, a state Senator, and an assortment of gamblers, writers, and racketeers, chief of which latter group was the amiable and gracious Mike Francesco, who operated the city's brothels and handbooks.

Sheila glanced down at her simple dark suit, and

nudged Jake sharply. "You bastard," she said, through a tight smile.

"You look wonderful. Colorless and self-effacing. People will think you're my cousin from What Cheer, Iowa."

Jake saw May then, seated cross-legged on a window seat and laughing with a hard-faced jockey and a gray haired man whom Jake didn't know.

She was sitting in what seemed to be an inconspicuous corner, but the grouping of the guests and the lines of the room drew attention to her inevitably. May had the talent of always being noticed and noticeable. She kept the spotlight on herself, no matter where she moved.

Sheila saw her too, and murmured, "Lovely, unaffected child, isn't she?"

Jake grinned. May was wearing a blue peasant skirt with a white blouse and ballet slippers, and her fabulous golden hair was worn long in Alice-in-Wonderland style.

Her legs which were crossed tailor fashion were bare, and she was leaning forward slightly with her elbows on her knees, in a childish but effective pose.

"All she needs is a gay little parasol," Sheila said.

"Oh, come off it. She's an artist at her business. Notice how overdressed everybody else looks?"

"As dear, sweet May knew they would."

May saw them standing in the archway then, and

waved a greeting. She stood up with a flash of bare legs, and skipped across to them.

"Jake," she said. "How wonderful." Putting a hand on Sheila's arm, in what seemed an afterthought, she said, "And you too, Sheila. Jake didn't say he was bringing you."

"No, he kept it a secret," Sheila said. "I wasn't in on it till we got into the cab."

"You poor dear, being dragged around like someone's aunt. And you look so sweet, too. Such a *really* simple suit."

Jake saw a touch of color in Sheila's cheeks and knew that May's comparatively gentle malice was not being wasted. Sheila started to say something, which would probably have been effective, but May circumvented that by laughing and turning to Jake.

Sheila let out her breath slowly, and said, "Excuse me, please. I see an old friend."

Alone with May, Jake said, "I'd like to talk to you a minute, in private. Okay?"

"This sounds exciting. Are you, at long last, going to make a pass at me?"

"No, this is important," he said, and smiled at the involuntary annoyance that showed in her face.

"All right," May said. "I'll see that everyone has drinks and we'll sneak up to the den of horror."

She moved away and Jake watched her, thinking that for all her good sense and humor she'd never been able to appreciate the fact that there might be men in the world who were not longing for her desperately.

May was delightful to look at, as she drifted from group to group, taking the focus of interest with her as she went. The fact that held everyone's attention on first meeting May, was the childish, pink-and-white freshness of her skin, and her air of enormous and vital health. Her eyes were light blue, almost lavender, and clear as mirrors; and although her body was slim, she created an impression of bland voluptuousness. May looked always as if she had just been massaged, bathed, perfumed, nourished, and rested, although in fact she could get along on four hours' sleep a night, while living to the hilt the remaining twenty hours. She had an indestructible set of glands, organs, ligaments and tissues, and the whole functioned like a beautiful, well-oiled machine.

Jake went to the buffet to get a drink. He nodded to several people he knew, and tried unsuccessfully to fend off an intense young man who wrote daytime radio serials. The young man, whose name was Rengale, was defensive about his work, but not reticent.

Jake nodded absently to his remarks, and glanced over to the divan where Sheila was sitting with a successful young magazine illustrator. The illustrator was talking animatedly, and it was obvious that he was delighted with Sheila.

Jake frowned and sipped his drink. His marriage

with Sheila hadn't worked. Sheila had called it off good-naturedly after two years that had seemed exceptionally pleasant to Jake.

They were still married, technically. Sheila had not yet filed for a divorce. But that was just a matter of time. Jake still didn't know what had been wrong. But he couldn't see that the break had been completely his fault.

Rengale, the radio writer, disrupted his nostalgic reflections by tapping him squarely on the chest with his forefinger.

"There's no room for argument," he said, making a gesture of contemptuous dismissal with his horn rimmed glasses. "The soap opera has become a whipping boy for Book-of-the-Month-Club intellectuals, and other members of the culturally *nouveau riche*, and now," Rengale paused for breath and twisted his lips into a sardonic sneer, "and now, it's a hallmark of the most utter sophistication to treat radio writers with the gentle tolerance more usually reserved for hydrocephalous adults. Because—"

"What are you writing now?" Jake said, wishing to hell May would come back.

Rengale brightened. "I'm doing a show for Mutual. Judy Trent, Copy Girl. It's about a copy girl, you know, who gets into one scrape after another."

"Good twist," Jake said, gravely.

"Actually it's not a bad show. The character of Judy,

as I've conceived her, is a nice blend of the insecurity and compensatory aggressiveness of this present generation." Rengale paused and looked thoughtfully at his pipe. "It's sustaining, at the present time, of course."

Jake saw with relief that May was coming toward him, but sighed as she was intercepted by Mike Francesca.

Mike Francesca was a small, thickly built man with curly gray hair and mild, twinkling blue eyes. His skin was deeply tanned and wrinkled, and when he smiled his face wreathed into a surprising criss-cross of lines and creases. He smiled a lot, and was unfailingly gentle and amiable in manner, even when forced by the demands of his profession to drop a cement-coated competitor into the Chicago River.

"We have not seen each other in much too long a time," Mike was saying.

"Well, whose fault is that?" May said.

Rengale was still pouring out his troubles, but Jake could hear the conversation between May and Mike Francesca quite clearly.

"Ah, my fault," Mike said, with an apologetic little bob of his head. "Today I lead a quiet, simple life out on my farm. I grow vegetables like my father did in Sicily, and my back has an ache in it that is very good. I dig in the ground, and drink a little wine, and go to bed early. It is very nice."

"My God, you sound like a bad story in the Saroyan manner," May said. "All this digging in the good clean earth, and drinking the clear red *vino*, and everything being so damn good. Really, Mike, it's ghastly."

Mike smiled without understanding. "I think you are not being very nice to an old man," he said.

"I'm a bitch, Mike. But I'm going to square myself with you when I write my book."

Mike continued to smile, but the warm, mobile good humor in his blunt brown features had disappeared. "Ah, I heard of this book, May. You will write about me, eh?"

"Mike, you're my star character. Everybody is dying to get the inside story on you."

"We had fun in the old days, eh, May? We talked a lot together, and no secrets between us, eh? Plenty of wine, plenty of talk. Maybe a little too much of both, I think."

"Are you trying in your tactful fashion to tell me something?" May said, laughing.

"Only this, because we are friends. Write your book, but don't hurt your old friends." Mike smiled gently. "I am an old man now, May. I want to live on my farm and enjoy everything in peace."

"You make it sound fetching."

Mike put a broad, leather-skinned hand on May's bare shoulder, and shook her slightly. "I am not one to go around saying woof! woof! to people. But I must ask you, please, to forget some of our talk, eh?"

"Okay, I'll forget some of it," May grinned. "But not all of it, Mike. Now you'll have to excuse me."

Turning quickly from him she waved at Jake. "Come on, I'm ready, lover."

Jake excused himself from Rengale and joined May. He nodded to Mike, whom he'd known for many years, and followed May through the archway and up the stairs to the second floor.

Reaching the landing Jake looked back down and saw Mike Francesca getting slowly into his coat in the foyer. The old man was alone and there was a distressed, thoughtful expression on his face. Jake was thinking as he followed May into her bedroom that he would not like to be the cause of that particular expression on Mike Francesca's face.

May settled herself comfortably on a chaise longue covered with pink brocade and crossed her slim legs at the ankles.

"Drink?" she said, nodding at a bottle-laden table beside the longue.

Jake sat down on a dainty three-legged chair and built two drinks. May sipped hers approvingly, and said, "Don't you like the Walden simplicity I've created up here?"

Glancing around, Jake grinned. The high-ceilinged bedroom faced east, but thick pink drapes were pulled together now shutting off the view of the park and the lake. White fur rugs were scattered about the polished floor, and the immense four-poster bed, covered with fat pink pillows, stood imposingly in the middle of the room. The light was soft, and there was a fireplace and bookshelves. May's dressing table was impressive as a tribal altar, with its flesh-toned mirrors, and the banks of crystal jars that contained hand lotions, cold creams, powders and colognes.

"You need a couple of blackamoors with ostrich fans," Jake said. "Outside of that you didn't miss a trick."

"It's cozy," May smiled.

"The very word for it." Jake lit a cigarette. "I managed to eavesdrop on your conversation with Francesca. Sounded grim. What's up?"

"Oh, nothing at all," May said. "Now, what's on your mind?"

"I hear you're writing a book."

"Ah, fame," May said, and smiled at the ceiling.

"My interest, as usual, is completely selfish. Dan Riordan has hired us to handle his press relations. He's worried about your book."

"He's got no reason to worry. Unless his heart isn't pure."

"He's got reason to worry then, I suppose."

"Jake, Riordan is somewhat of a bastard. I'm a little surprised that you're mixed up with him."

Jake smiled. "You're out of character. Let's go back

a bit. Do you have anything on Riordan?"

"Assuming I have. What then?"

"Are you going to use it?"

"I will if it adds to the story."

"The book is no gag, then? You're going ahead with it?"

"Nothing will stop me from writing this book," May said quietly.

Jake shook his head. "I don't get it, frankly. You're going out of your way to stick your chin out. I yield to no one in my admiration for good, clean fun, but irritating men like Mike Francesca and Dan Riordan comes under another heading. Why are you doing it?"

"The usual, shoddy reasons," May said coolly. "Money, prestige, and so forth. You're being a bore, Jake."

"Okay. Tell me something about the book then."

May smiled dreamily. "Jake, it's going to be a classic. It will be autobiography in the grand French manner." She widened her eyes innocently, and said, "That's why I can't be too concerned with the personal feelings of the people involved, even if one of them happens to be your client."

Jake grinned at her. "Don't give me that 'grand French tradition' business. I knew you when you thought Hemingway played third for the Cubs."

May laughed good-naturedly. "You're the one person I can't impress."

"Where and how did you get the information on people like Riordan?"

May sat up, and lifted a foot-square, black lacquered box from the coffee table. She opened it and removed a thick, leather-bound book. "Here's where the bodies are buried."

"Well, well. The good, old-fashioned diary with all the shoddy dope. I haven't seen one since I stopped covering murders. They're awfully old hat now."

"Oh, this one just covers the war years. I've gone modern since then. Anyway, I have all the little tidbits I need right here."

"Well, good luck," Jake sighed. He saw no point in talking with her now. Perhaps later he could point out to her that she was making a mistake, at least, he thought cynically, so far as Riordan was concerned.

May put the diary away and went downstairs where she was reclaimed by the jockey, who led her aggressively to the bar.

Jake stood by himself, smoking a cigarette, and gradually he began to sense a curious feeling in the air. He saw that most of the men, and several of the women, had turned when May entered the room, and were watching her now as she walked to the bar with the jockey.

They made a comical picture. The jockey was two inches shorter than May, but his body was like something made of leather and wire. May's Alice-in-

Wonderland hair, and her absurdly simple clothes, made her look like a cheerful, innocent child walking with the toughest boy in the neighborhood.

For some reason no one seemed amused by May at the moment, and in the strange silence that followed her entrance, Jake noticed definite tension in the room.

It was fear, he realized with a start. Most of the people in the room were afraid of something.

He smiled at that thought, because it seemed so melodramatic and unlikely; but then he noticed troubled expressions on several faces, and the speculative way many of the men watched May; and that, plus the odd silence and the nervous shifting about of a few people, made him realize that his first, instinctive judgment had been right.

There was fear in the room, and it was fear of May.

Sheila came over to him and asked if he was ready to leave. He said all right and started to tell her what he had noticed; but the mood of the room had changed by that time. He wondered if his imagination was becoming overactive and decided to keep still.

The knocker sounded as Jake helped her into her coat in the foyer. The maid hurried past them and opened the door.

Dan Riordan and Gary Noble walked in and Gary did a double-take on seeing Jake. But he seemed pleased, and Jake guessed it was because it would indicate to Riordan that the agency was wasting no time.

Riordan nodded to Sheila as Jake made the introductions. Then he said, "Have you talked with May?"

"Yes."

Riordan said, "Did she mention me?"

"I did," Jake said. "She hinted that she might have something—" He paused, looking for a tactful word, then gave it up and said, "She's got something on you, or thinks she has, but we didn't get too specific."

Riordan took a long, deliberate breath, and then nodded jerkily at Sheila and strode toward the parlor.

"I'll stick with him," Noble said. "He called me after you left, said he wanted to see May tonight. He's a stubborn character."

"We were leaving, remember?" Sheila said.

They found a cab outside and started for Dave's.

"Why the frown?" Sheila said quietly, as Jake fumbled for cigarettes.

"May. She's drifting into trouble. And I'll be damned if I see why. I just can't figure it out."

He told her what he had learned from May, and they talked about it that night until Sheila yawned pointedly, and Jake changed the subject.

CHAPTER THREE

JAKE reached the office at ten the next morning. The receptionist said Noble wished to see him right away, so Jake walked down to his office. Noble was at the bar and looked unhappy. But he brightened when Jake came in.

"Care for a drink?" he said.

Jake said no and sat down beside Noble's desk. "What's up?"

"Well, the session with May last night accomplished very little." Noble brought the drink to his desk and sat down in his leather-backed swivel chair. "Damn that woman," he said in the voice one would use to damn the weather, or any other disagreeable but inevitable phenomenon. "She seemed to go out of her way to antagonize Riordan. I never pretended to understand her, but now, by God, I don't think anyone can."

"What happened?"

Noble lit a cigarette and ran a hand through his rumpled white hair. "The bare facts won't give you an idea of the way it was." Noble waved a hand futilely. "It was as if she were the only one there who wasn't afraid of something."

"I think I know what you mean. Go on."

"Riordan wasn't in a good mood, in the first place. He picked me up at the office and didn't talk on the way to May's. He barged into May's parlor and told her he wanted to talk with her."

Noble put out his cigarette, then lit another and frowned at the curling smoke. "I can't describe it very well," he said. "But the impression I got was that May was deliberately trying to be as bitchy as possible. He asked about her book, and she immediately expressed vast surprise that he cared about literature. Riordan knew he was being laughed at. But he stuck his ground. He said he'd heard about the book and that he hoped she wasn't using anything which he'd told her in confidence."

Jake said, "Was everybody at the party listening to this?"

"Hard to say. Neither of them raised their voices, but I suppose they could have been overheard if anyone bothered to listen. Anyway, May kept needling Riordan, but she did it in that good humored, little-girl manner she affects at times. She asked him what he was worried about, and from her attitude you might think she really didn't know."

"Well, what *is* Riordan worried about?" Jake said.

"This vague talk of exposés and so forth is unconvincing as hell. Does May have something specific and damaging on him?"

"I don't know. He acts as if she did. Last night I got the impression he would enjoy strangling her, slowly and carefully."

"How did their talk end?"

"It didn't really end, in the sense that anything was settled. Riordan warned her not to use anything about him, said she'd be making a mistake. May pretended to believe he was referring to the artistic problems of selection, and so forth, and assured him she would be most careful in her choice of incidents. She told him very sweetly that biography in the de Sévigné manner was a form that required a blending of techniques at their highest level of effectiveness, and that any mistake she made would only be because she aspired too high. She laughed then and said he probably hadn't the vaguest idea of what she was talking about, and added that this was not at all surprising considering his bourgeois predilections."

"Nice sweet exit line," Jake said.

Noble shrugged and sipped his drink. "Riordan is mad as hell, Jake. He's going to be hard to handle."

"Let's not worry about that. Isn't his man due here this morning with some facts and figures?"

"I forgot. Riordan called this morning and said Avery Meed—that's his secretary—couldn't make it today, but will be here tomorrow morning. That gives us a day's grace."

The phone on Noble's desk buzzed. He lifted it, listened, then handed it to Jake. "For you."

Jake said, "Hello."

There was a pause. Then: "Jake, it's May. I have melodramatic news right out of a grade B thriller. Someone tried to break into my little bagnio early this morning. Isn't that interesting?"

"That's nothing funny," Jake said.

"It's hardly tragic, however," May said. "What I called for was to see if you could have coffee with me this morning. I feel in the mood for you. How about it?"

"Sure, I'll come right over."

Jake hung up, glanced at Noble. "Someone tried to break into May's last night."

"She's a damn idiot," Noble said shortly. "She'll get into trouble and make a mess for everyone. You know how the papers would love to latch onto her tie-up with Riordan? That would shoot our campaign right in the tail."

"I'm going out to have breakfast with her now," Jake said. "Maybe this is a good thing. It might frighten her into using her head."

The cab ride to May's was pleasant. The colors were changing in the shrubs and trees of the park, and the gray fall waters of the lake were smooth as slate except for occasional lacy whitecaps.

May met him at the door and led him to her study, which was on the first floor, facing the morning sun. It was a brisk room, done in white leather, and furnished with deep chairs, an enormous coffee table, and a desk piled high with books and manuscript. A silver coffee service was on the coffee table, and the white Venetian blinds were drawn against the morning sun. The room was pleasantly dim.

May wore a simple gray dress with gray suède shoes, and her heavy, shining hair was looped up into a low chignon. Her eyes were clear, and her skin was fresh and blooming. She looked like an enormously healthy and beautiful school teacher who bought her clothes in Paris.

She poured coffee, sitting beside Jake on the deep couch. A bar of sunlight struck her face and she put her hand up in a curious, defensive gesture. Jake saw then that she was tired; there were tiny lines at the corners of her eyes and mouth and the illusion of her glowing youth was shaken for an instant. She stood up quickly and adjusted the blind. Then she sat down beside Jake again.

"I hate sunlight," she said, irritably.

"What about last night? I didn't rush over here to hear about your phobias."

May told the story simply. She had gone to bed at two o'clock, the maid having left. She stayed alone at night until the cleaning woman, a Mrs. Swenson, came in at six in the morning, May explained digressively. Sometime after falling asleep she was awakened by a sound on the first floor. The time was three fifteen. She came downstairs and snapped on the lights. There was no one in the house. But an attempt had been made to force a window on the side of the house. A pane of glass had been broken. Her arrival probably scared off whoever had been trying to get in.

"Well, what do you think?" she asked, smiling. "White slavers, maybe?"

"Has it occurred to you that someone may be worried about this book you're planning?" Jake said, drily.

"Oh, don't be ridiculous!"

"Listen: I heard Mike Francesca talking last night and I know he's not happy. Also Dan Riordan is stewing about your book. And there are probably others. So don't tell me I'm ridiculous."

"How do you know about Riordan?"

"Noble told me this morning. You weren't very nice to our client, I gather."

May laughed and then lit a cigarette. "That was my sincerest hope," she said. "Jake, Riordan is a type I dislike. He's the perfect symbol of our society today, the insane blending of Geiger counters with animated commercials. He's a mixture of man and child, at home building a million dollar plant but equally in character smashing all the furniture with a hammer."

"I never suspected your flair for epigram," Jake said. "But the fact that Riordan conforms to our culture is no reason to crucify him."

"Do I have to have a reason for everything?" May said sharply. Standing, she walked to the window and her shoulders were straight and angry.

Jake remembered that she had been annoyed last night when he'd pressed her about her reasons for writing the book. He lit a cigarette and tried to guess what that reaction meant. Finally a thought occurred to him that seemed to supply the answer, but its very obviousness made him suspicious.

"Turn around and stop sulking," he said. "I'm curious about why you're writing this book. You don't need money, and you aren't yearning for literary recognition. So what's left?"

May came back and sat beside him. She crossed her beautiful legs and leaned back comfortably, apparently in better spirits. "What difference does it make why I write the book?"

"None, I suppose," Jake said. "But I'm curious. You're going to hurt people, you're going to make enemies. Why go to all that trouble to become unpopular?"

"Embarrassing a collection of charlatans and frauds is no trouble," May said, grinning.

"They were your friends at one time."

"Such magnificent friends they were," May said.

She crushed out her cigarette and looked down at her hands. "Let's don't talk about it any more."

"Okay," Jake said.

The door opened as he was preparing to say good-bye; the maid came in and said, "There's a man and woman to see you, Miss Laval. A Mr. and Mrs. Riordan."

"Well, well," Jake said.

"Show them in," May said, grinning at Jake.

The maid reappeared a moment later and stepped aside at the doorway. Denise Riordan walked in, looking tanned and sure of herself in voluptuous mink, but the man with her wasn't Dan Riordan. It was his lean, sandy-haired son, Brian.

Brian grinned at Jake and walked over to shake hands. Jake introduced him and Denise to May.

"We were having coffee," May said. "Would you like something stronger, Mrs. Riordan?"

"No, thank you. I sometimes go all the way until the afternoon without a drink," Denise said drily.

Brian said, "I'll take a whiskey and soda, if you don't mind." He put a hand to his forehead gingerly. "Last night was Homeric in a sloppy sort of way."

Denise sat in a chair opposite the sofa, where bars of the clean morning sun highlighted the perfection of her furs. She was wearing a brown suit, with alligator pumps. There was a controlled, deliberate quality about her, Jake noticed, as she lighted a cigarette.

She watched May all the time, studying her as if she were some curious phenomenon that had been brought to her attention for the first time.

Finally she said, "Dan has told me a lot about you, Miss Laval."

May smiled gently as she poured coffee, and Jake decided she had already taken a round from Denise. Her simple gray suit and relaxed manner made Riordan's wife, for all her polished beauty, look like a burlesque queen.

"Dear Danny," May said. "So impulsive and . . ." She paused, considering a word. "So garrulous," she concluded. "What did he tell you about me?"

The maid brought Brian his drink, and he sipped it gratefully. "Fine," he said. "The old man told me about you, too," he said to May. "He had a great respect for your intelligence."

"I think 'shrewdness' was his word," Denise said, and blew smoke in the air.

"You mustn't give me too much credit," May said blandly. "Danny stands in awe of anyone who can read without moving his lips. But now that you've reminded me, Danny used to tell me about you, Denise. You were in show business or something, I believe."

"I was a dancer."

"Yes, I remember. Weren't you ever afraid of falling off the runway?" May said, innocently.

Brian Riordan slapped his thigh and let out a delighted shout. "Wonderful, wonderful," he said, beaming at Denise.

Denise looked at him without expression. She put out her cigarette with a hard vicious gesture, and turned to May. "I didn't come here to swap wise-cracks," she said.

"You haven't, of course," May smiled. "But go on."

"Dan is worried over what you're going to write about him," Denise said, and now there were spots of angry color in her cheeks. "He didn't send me to see you, if that's what you're thinking. I came on my own because he means a lot to me. Can you understand that?"

"Why, of course, my dear," May said.

"All right. I want you to let him alone. We've had a good time of it so far, and I don't want everything spoiled."

May sipped her coffee for a moment in silence. Finally she glanced at Brian. "May I ask why you came here?"

"Not at all," Brian said. He smiled. "I came to re-phrase my step-mother's comments, which I knew would be inadequate. Let me put it this way: I have no illusions about my father. However, there is enough of his money around to take care of everyone in his circle very nicely. I like that. So does Denise. So, I should think, would you. Do you see what I mean?"

"All too clearly," May said.

"I like things clearly understood," Denise said quietly and it seemed she had recovered her poise. "We'll pay you to destroy whatever damaging records or information you have about Dan. That leaves one thing to settle: How much?"

May stood up and Jake saw that she was angry, beautifully and completely angry.

She said to Brian, "You came here to re-phrase your step-mother's comments. You bungled the job. This overdressed creature," she said, swinging about suddenly and pointing at Denise, "who, I might add, blackmailed your father into marriage by feigning a maidenly hysteria at the prospects of a pregnancy which, after the wedding, turned out to be a false alarm, has about as much understanding of my work as a grub in a bag. She's worried about her meal ticket. She'd have to go back to doing the grinds if anything happened to Dan Riordan."

May raised her hand imperiously as Denise got to her feet, trembling with anger. "Don't lose control of yourself," she said coolly. "I am writing a book which interests me and which will be finished quite soon. It's a work of art quite outside your comprehensions, which are limited to eating, sleeping and lusting, I presume. The fact that your husband is an integral piece in the mosaic I am doing is unfortunate. For you, that is."

"Just a minute," Brian said, gently. He patted Denise's shoulder in a soothing gesture before turning to May. "I love all this fine rhetoric," he said, "but I don't believe in it. I never heard a writer talk about an 'integral piece in his mosaics.' You're not kidding me, May."

"Oh, Lord!" May said, with mock despair. "Now the sophomores have figured me out, Jake."

"I'm no sophomore," Brian said, still smiling. "I've been through a big war, and I've seen girls with their clothes off, and I've filled an inside straight flush. But that's beside the point. I think you should stop acting and listen to my proposition."

May lit a cigarette with an annoyed gesture, then sat on the couch and slumped back against the cushions. Letting the cigarette dangle from her lips she put her feet up on the coffee table and looked at Denise and Brian through the curling smoke.

"Please go home," she said. "Say that wonderful word 'goodbye' and get the hell out of here."

"Let's go," Brian said shortly.

Denise glared down at May and there was naked hatred in her face. "You'll regret this, you bitch," she said.

"Goodbye, my dear," May said, languidly. "And by the way, ask Danny sometime about that girl in Amarillo. She was a Minsky grad, too. Maybe you knew each other."

Denise walked out of the room and Brian, after an amused salute to May, followed her. Jake smoked in silence until he heard the front door close. Then he said, "You were in good form. All part of your unpopularity program, I take it?"

"I don't know what the hell it's part of," May said in a musing voice. She lifted one leg about a foot above the coffee table and turned her neatly shod foot about in a slow circle. "That's a very good ankle, if I say so myself," she said.

Jake stood and glanced at his watch. "I've got to run along, May."

May came to the front door with him, and the maid brought his hat and gloves. Jake opened the door and in the bright sudden light he saw that May looked tired and old. She stepped away from the sun and put a hand to her face.

"You look tired," he said.

"You look like a Dachau escape yourself," she said sharply.

"Oh, come off it. Get some rest and you'll be all right. And one other thing. Take care of yourself, will you? Do you have anyone here with you at night?"

"No, the maid leaves after dinner. Mrs. Swenson comes in at six or seven in the morning."

"Why don't you ask her to sleep in?"

"Because I don't want anyone in the house when I'm working. I don't like people tiptoeing around and eavesdropping." She gave him a little push toward the door. "Come on. Don't hang around on the slim chance that a good exit line will occur to you."

Jake grinned and patted her shoulder. She smiled at him as he went down the steps and when he reached the sidewalk he turned and they waved to each other.

That afternoon Jake tried to get some work done on an industrial account the agency had got recently. The company, which was having union trouble, wanted a brochure for distribution to its retailers which would puff its products while implying that such achievements could be made only in an open shop.

It was very dull, and Jake found his thoughts wandering time and again to May, and the trouble she represented for him, and the people she intended to write about.

He had a hunch why she was planning to write the book. She needed attention and she was trying desperately to get it. Through a combination of factors she had lost the excitement and limelight after the war. Her friends were scattered, she was alone. May was no longer the radiant, compelling woman she had once been; in the cheerful pastel lighting of her home she was still lovely, but the reckless, untended beauty had gone. That beauty had been a magnet and people had forgiven May a great deal because of it.

Her tragedy was that she couldn't change her values, or accept the change in herself. She was growing old and felt she was being shunted aside. That, he guessed, accounted for her touchiness about why she was writing the book. She was ashamed of what she was doing, and why she was doing it.

The pettiness of May's motivation didn't surprise Jake, because he had long ago decided that many of the lovely or ugly things men did had their origin in incongruously mean causes. Men fashioned towering philosophies to justify what ignorant nurses had told them as children, and great books and plays had been written because the authors hadn't made athletic teams or had acne. These insignificant irritants worked on the human soul like a grain of sand in a bivalve, and the results were things of great beauty or terror.

Jake thought about it that afternoon and got very little work done. He called Sheila at six to ask her to have dinner with him, but she had a date. He dined alone and returned to his club about eight thirty, where he read several current magazines before showering and going to bed.

That was at one thirty.

CHAPTER FOUR

THE phone waked him the next morning. He put it against his ear without raising his head from the pillow. "Yes?"

"Jake?" It was Gary Noble's voice, oddly strained. "Jake, May was killed last night. . . . Can you hear me?"

"Oh, God," Jake said. He swung his feet from under the covers and came up to a sitting position, fully awake. "What happened?"

"She was killed—in her home early this morning. Jake, what the devil will this mean to us?"

Jake glanced at his bedside clock. Seven thirty. He lit a cigarette. He was conscious of not thinking clearly, or rather, of not thinking at all.

"Jake?"

"I'm still here," Jake said. "How did you find out?"

"It was on the seven o'clock broadcast. Jake, you'd better run out to her place and see what the police are thinking."

"Okay," Jake said.

"And Jake. Don't mention anything about Riordan and May to the police."

"Oh, for God's sake," Jake said.

"I'm just reminding you."

"Okay, I'll meet you in the office later."

From Jake's club on Michigan Boulevard to May's apartment was a ten minute cab ride. When he arrived he saw a small group of men and women on the sidewalk, and two police cars parked before her home. The whispering crowd regarded Jake with speculative curiosity as he went up the stone steps to where a uniformed policeman was on guard at the door.

"Hold it," the patrolman said.

"Who's here from Homicide?" Jake asked.

"Lieutenant Martin."

"Would you tell him Jake Harrison would like to see him? I think it will be okay."

The policeman shrugged but went inside. Returning a few seconds later he gave Jake a look of grudging respect. "Go on in," he said.

Lieutenant Martin was standing alone in the foyer. He smiled at Jake and they shook hands.

"What brings you here?" Martin said.

"Nothing, but May was a friend of mine. What happened?"

Lieutenant Martin rested an elbow against the curved bannister and rubbed his chin.

"She was killed sometime this morning, around four,

if you want a guess. That's about all we know."

Jake realized as he listened to Martin's flat casual voice, that subconsciously he hadn't believed Noble; he hadn't believed that May was dead. Now he felt the shock of Martin's cold and final words as if he were receiving the news for the first time.

He stood with Martin in the gray morning light remembering that he had stood in the same place with May the day before, after Denise and Brian Riordan had gone. She had been cheerful as they said goodbye.

"She was a good friend, eh?" Martin said.

"I liked her. I hadn't seen much of her for the last couple of years, but I—she was an honest, likeable person." He stopped unable to think of words that were not empty or inane.

"Well, it's a weird case," Martin said.

"What do you mean?"

"Come on upstairs. You'll see what I mean."

Jake had know Martin for fifteen years, dating back to when he had covered police for the *Herald-Messenger,* and Martin had been a detective working out of the third division in South Chicago. He knew Martin to be patient, painstaking, and thorough, with a passion for orderly police work. Most important, he had imagination. He was not afraid to guess and play his hunches.

Martin stopped at the head of the stairs to let three photographers by, and then turned and went into

May's bedroom.

Jake followed him slowly.

The figure on the bed had nothing to do with May, Jake told himself. May was gone. This sprawled and staring thing with the black sash imbedded deeply in the flesh of its throat was something else.

Rationalizing didn't help and Jake could feel perspiration starting on his face. She had been wearing a billowing, black lace negligee and high-heeled black mules. One leg was doubled back beneath her body and one slipper had fallen off and was lying on its side on the floor. The black silken sash about her throat was obviously the belt she had worn with the negligee.

"See what I mean?" Martin said.

Jake saw he wasn't looking at the bed. He was looking beyond the bed. Following his eyes Jake saw that the pink-toned mirror above May's dressing table had been marked with two large X's drawn with bright red lipstick. Cologne and perfume bottles had been swept from the dresser top to the floor, and clothes had been pulled from the closets and strewn over the floor and furniture. It looked as if a madman had attacked the place.

"What do you make of that?" Martin said.

Jake shook his head. "You have any ideas?"

"Only guesses. The X's could mean that the murderer was referring to a double-cross." He glanced at Jake and smiled faintly. "Too pat, I think. Someone might have been looking for something, of course, or it could be that the murderer felt killing her wasn't enough. You know, a form of mutilation."

Jake remembered then that May had kept her diary in this room. She had shown it to him the night before last, at her party.

He glanced over to the coffee table and saw that the lacquered box in which she'd kept it was closed. Crossing the room, he opened the box and saw, without much surprise, that it was empty.

The record of May's wartime gossip, and the activities of quite a few prominent men, including Dan Riordan, had disappeared.

Martin came over, looking interested. "What're you looking for?"

Jake knew that Martin would eventually learn of the book May had been planning, and of Dan Riordan and other prominent men who weren't happy about the idea.

So he told Martin everything he knew.

Martin nodded slowly. "We'll look for that diary now. You're working for Riordan. Maybe you know where he was this morning about four o'clock."

"Haven't any idea. You're fairly sure of the time?"

"Fairly sure," Martin said, as they walked to the door. "The body was discovered by a Mrs. Swenson, a cleaning woman who got here at six. She told us that she went out to mail some stuff that was in the hall, and when she came back and went upstairs she found her mistress dead."

"Did she lock the door when she went out?"

"No, but there's no chance that someone slipped in and did the job while she was away. The coroner definitely put it before four thirty, and after three."

Downstairs Jake shook hands with Martin and was turning to leave when he saw two men coming up the steps.

The policeman on guard stopped them, and said, "Nobody goes in now."

The man in the lead said, "Tell the officer in charge I'd like to see him."

Martin walked to the doorway. "What can I do for you?" he said.

"Are you in charge?"

"Yes. Martin's the name. Lieutenant Martin."

The man said, "My name is Prior, Gregory Prior, chief of the legal staff of the Hampstead Committee. This is my assistant, Gil Coombs. I had an appointment with Miss Laval for ten o'clock this morning. Mr. Coombs heard on the radio that she had been murdered, so we came right out."

"I see," Martin said agreeably. "What kind of business did you have with her?"

Jake studied Prior with interest. This was the government agent making the initial investigation into Riordan's books and contracts. He looked young for the job, about thirty-four or thirty-five, with thick brown hair, and a firm, intelligent face.

Prior said, "I can only tell you this much: Miss Laval called my assistant, Mr. Coombs, last night about twelve and told him that she wanted to get in touch with me. I called her back later. She said she had some information I might be interested in, and we made an appointment for ten this morning."

"The information was in her diary, I think," Martin said. "Is that right?"

Prior didn't look surprised by Martin's information. He said, "That's what she told me on the phone."

"The diary seems to be gone," Martin said. "Anyway, it's not in its usual place. I'm going to look around for it now, and you can join me if you like."

"Thank you," Prior said.

Two policemen came in with a stretcher and started up the stairs. Martin said, "I'll be with you in a moment," and went up after them.

Prior lit a cigarette and then glanced curiously at Jake. Jake said, "We'll meet eventually, Mr. Prior, so why not now? My name is Jake Harrison."

"Yes?" Prior said.

"I'm handling Dan Riordan's public relations," Jake said, and extended his hand.

"Oh," Prior said. He didn't offer to shake hands.

Jake put his hand into his breast pocket and brought out cigarettes. "I'm surprised that May had decided to turn over her dope on Riordan to you," he said. "You know, she said she was going to use it in a book."

"Well, she didn't say anything about turning over the information," Coombs said. He was a thin, middle-aged man with alert features. "She merely asked me to tell Prior she wanted to talk to him."

"She didn't say the information concerned Riordan," Prior said.

Coombs said, "But we were hoping this might give us a lead to—"

Prior cleared his throat. "Hardly the place for that, Gil."

Coombs colored and nodded. "Sorry," he said.

"I hope you won't think of me as the guy on the other team," Jake said. He lit the cigarette he held in his hand and wondered to what extent he could soften up Prior. The man seemed sincere and earnest, and there was a chance he might be reasonable.

"Actually our jobs are pretty similar," he went on. "You want to get the facts, and my job is to pass those facts along to the public, and to see that they don't become distorted on the way. I'll be glad to help you any way I can in regard to Riordan's background, activities, and so forth. Frankly, I want your confidence and cooperation, because my job is not to defend Riordan, but to keep him from being libeled by the implications of this investigation."

"We aren't sensation mongers, Mr. Harrison," Prior

said. "We aren't interested in anything but cold facts."

"That makes me feel better," Jake said, and did his best to appear ingenuously relieved. "And, off the record, I think you'll find that Riordan did just about what any other business man would have done, and what hundreds of them did, as a matter of fact. After all, we were at war and the pressure was on everyone to get stuff out of the factories and overseas. Cutting corners was a national pastime."

"Perhaps," Prior said, noncommittally; and seemed to withdraw into his shell, so Jake stopped pressing. He shook hands with both men and left.

He got to the office twenty minutes later, at about eight forty-five, and went in to see Noble. He related briefly what had happened; and added that he'd told Martin that Riordan was probably featured in May's diary.

Noble ran a hand through his disarranged hair and peered reproachfully at Jake. "Why the devil did you do that?"

"He'd have found it out anyway."

"I suppose." Noble went to the bar for a drink.

Jake lit a cigarette. "Big night?" he asked.

Noble nodded. He came back to his desk and Jake noted that he hadn't shaved, and his collar was wrinkled and soiled.

Jake said, "How do you know that Riordan had nothing to do with May's death?"

"I'm just hoping he didn't. The account wouldn't be worth a dime if Riordan went to the chair."

"That's a very objective way to look at it," Jake said. "You haven't heard from him by any chance?"

"Not a word. I talked to his wife, and she didn't know where he was."

Jake shrugged and walked to the door with Noble at his heels. "One thing, Jake," Noble said. "I—I'm going to need your help. I didn't go home last night. I—I'd appreciate it a lot if you'd back me up on a story that I spent the night with you."

"That's a great idea," Jake said. He saw that Noble was actually shaky, that his normally bronzed complexion had an undercast of green. "Where were you last night?"

"I told my wife I was tied up in a business meeting," Noble said, lowering his voice. "Actually I dropped in to see a friend of mine at the Regis Hotel. She's a grand girl, Jake, a grand girl, and if you knew her you'd know what I mean."

"Thank God I don't. What's her name?"

"Bebe Passione. That's a stage name, of course."

"Really? Gary, you're beyond me, at times. There's a murder investigation under way and you, along with quite a few other people, may have to explain where you were at four o'clock this morning. Do you understand that?"

"I know, I know," Noble said hastily. "That's just it.

If I tell the police I was with Bebe, then my wife will go melodramatically berserk. Don't you get it?"

"Sure, but I'm afraid I'll get it right in the neck." Jake patted Gary on the shoulder. "The answer, in a word, is 'No.' I'd like to help, but this isn't some collegiate prank, this is murder."

"Well, all right," Noble sighed. "Maybe the police won't be interested in where I was this morning. Maybe it will all blow over."

"Very likely," Jake said.

Jake walked down to his office and sat down at his desk; but after fiddling idly with a letter opener, he propped his feet on the desk and tried to think.

From his position he could look through the open door into the adjoining office, which was occupied by a girl named Toni Ryerson who had come to Noble's fresh from a night school course in public relations. Now he could see that she had her feet on her desk, too, giving him a nice view of her silken ankles. He got up and went into her office. Toni was reading a page of copy and holding a carton of coffee in her free hand. She was a thin, intense girl, with straight black hair, and an expression of brooding concentration.

"Hello, Jake," she said. "Did you hear the news?"

"Yes."

"Isn't it the damnedest thing you ever heard of? I've worked ten weeks on the Grant account, and this morning Noble sends me a memo that I'm being taken off it and put in the fashion department."

"Oh, that news," Jake said. "No, I hadn't heard about it. A memo, eh? That's pretty rough. You'd think he'd have called you in and given you a last cigarette and a blindfold before the *coup de grâce*. Did he say why?"

"I guess he just had a brainstorm."

"Well, you've got to expect things like that. This is the fabulous business world, you know. There's no point in calling Gary a fathead. That's obvious, because if he had any brains he'd get out and start an agency of his own instead of working for us."

Toni smiled. "I guess everything does happen for the best."

Jake wondered without any real curiosity what Toni would do without her stock of protective aphorisms. She was one of that happy breed who pad their egos with a thick coating of clichés, apothegms, quotations and saws to serve as a buffer between themselves and reality. There was no failure, no humiliation, no circumstance, that Toni could not hopefully reassess in the light of what someone had said, more or less truthfully, in the distant past.

Dean Niccolo came in through the other door wearing tweeds and a pipe, and Jake noticed that Toni brightened up immediately.

Niccolo said to Jake, "Too bad about May. I just saw the news."

"What's all this?" Toni said.

"May Laval, a friend of ours, was killed this morning," Jake said.

"Good gosh," Toni said. "You know, when I saw the kind of weather we had this morning, I said, 'What a day for a murder.' Isn't that odd?"

"Not really," Jake said, and Toni looked at him blankly.

Niccolo sat down in the chair beside Toni's desk and ran a hand through his thick, dark hair. His features were moody as he stared at the tips of his heavy brogues. "I didn't know her very well, just bumped into her a few times around town. But she was a good egg. The police have any ideas yet?"

Jake said no, and then excused himself and returned to his own office. He guessed from the happy glow on Toni's face that she'd appreciate an interlude alone with Niccolo, so he closed the connecting door between their offices.

Jake's phone buzzed. Picking it up he learned that Mr. Avery Meed, from Mr. Riordan's office, was waiting to see him. Jake told the receptionist to send him right in. When he put the phone down he saw that Sheila was standing in the doorway. She smiled and came to his side and put the back of her hand against his cheek.

"I heard about May," she said. "I'm sorry, Jake."

He squeezed her hand. "Thanks. I feel pretty low

about it."

She picked up his desk lighter and held a flame to the cigarette he put in his mouth. "Would you like to go out and get drunk?"

"No, I've got work to do. But it's the best offer I've had all morning."

"Jake, I'm sorry for the things I said about her the other night."

"I know. You were mad at me, not her."

There was a dry cough from the doorway. Jake glanced up and saw a neatly dressed man standing there, a brief case under his arm, and a politely expressionless look on his face.

"I am Avery Meed," he said.

"Oh, come in," Jake said. He introduced Avery Meed to Sheila, who excused herself and left.

Meed sat down in the leather arm chair beside Jake's desk, his feet planted squarely together on the floor, the brief case resting on his lap. He was past fifty, Jake judged, but his small body was firm and his eyes were alert. He wore a suit of banker's gray that bore the expensively dowdy stamp of Brooks Brothers, and a high starched collar with a black knit tie. There was an air of attentiveness about him, as if he were waiting for a command.

Jake said, "Mr. Riordan told us you could give us a picture of what we're going to be up against in this investigation. I'm an ignoramus about figures, so don't expect too much from me."

Meed smiled mechanically. "I will try to clarify any points you find confusing." Zippering open his brief case he placed two manila folders before Jake. "These statements cover the operations of the Riordan Mills and the Riordan Casting Company through 1943–1945."

Jake leafed through the two folders and saw that each contained summations of the various transactions, liabilities, assets, and balances of the two companies. The statement of net profit in each case was impressive.

"You did okay during the war," he said.

"Yes," Meed said.

Jake closed the folders. "Frankly, these things don't help much. Riordan told us the other night he had arbitrarily ignored certain government specifications in casting gun barrels. Is that all he did?"

"Basically, that is what happened."

"Then the government is likely to call him a crook, I imagine."

Meed smiled. "The government has to prove that. You know what happened because Mr. Riordan was frank with you; but we don't need to be so frank with the government."

"How about the companies' books? Won't they tell the story?"

Meed's smile was pleased. "Books, Mr. Harrison,

can tell many stories. You see, a set of books, kept with diligence and imagination, is in some respects like a dense, unmapped forest—quite impassable unless one knows where to look for trail markings."

"I see. Now check me if I'm wrong. Riordan deliberately used a cheaper grade of steel than specified in his contract, but the government men aren't likely to find that out from your official records. Is that right?"

"Yes."

"Then how did the Hampstead Committee get on Riordan's trail in the first place?"

Meed shrugged his neat shoulders.

"There were several cases of premature detonation in barrels cast by our firm. I believe some personnel were killed in at least two of the accidents. Reports made out by company commanders and ordnance inspectors took a long time to reach a level where they could be examined with any effect, but inevitably that happened, and the Riordan Casting Company was discovered to be the maker of the defective barrels. Hence this investigation."

Jake leaned back in his chair and fiddled with a pencil. Then he glanced at Meed. "What's your personal idea about this? I mean, do you think Riordan was justified in using cheap steel considering that men were killed as a result of that action?"

Meed appeared surprised. "I have no opinions on the subject," he said. "Perhaps," he added, smiling,

"I'm an unemotional man. The unnecessary death of American soldiers was an unhappy development, of course, but I see little point in applying moral terminology to the situation. The facts exist in a different light for everyone. Take the soldiers, for example— the fact of their death means one thing to their families; to me, it means a complication in the running of an industrial concern. I would be called heartless for that attitude, but that wouldn't change my feelings, you see."

"I see," Jake said drily. "No one could accuse you of letting your heart guide your head. But tell me this: Do you know a woman named May Laval?"

Meed paused. Then he said, "No, I never had that pleasure. I understand from this morning's papers that I never will."

"Maybe you know she had a diary supposed to contain information about Riordan."

"Yes, I knew that."

"Well, the diary has disappeared. Supposing it turns up. What then?"

"I see what you mean. Yes, the information in the diary might provide a clue to this investigating committee. That is a chance we must take, since there's nothing else we can do about it."

Jake realized that he had learned little from Meed. But it was encouraging to know that the facts of Riordan's manipulations were safely buried in labyrinthine records. The harder the body was to find the longer they could insist that there wasn't one in the first place.

As Meed was replacing the folders in his brief case, Jake said, "By the way, do you know where Riordan was this morning—early, I mean? About four, say."

Meed looked directly at Jake and smiled. "Oh, yes. Mr. Riordan was called to Gary, Indiana, last night. He stayed over until this morning with his plant manager."

Noble could relax now, Jake thought.

Niccolo walked in as Meed was preparing to leave. Jake introduced them, and Meed smiled impersonally, then excused himself and left.

"Who was that?" Niccolo said.

"One of Riordan's smooth little cogs," Jake said. "Avery Meed. Very sharp."

"That's good," Niccolo said. "We need brains on our side. I'll see you around."

When he left, Jake strolled to the windows and stared down at the magnificent panorama of the city, unreal and mysterious in the smoky fall weather. From the height of his office he could see the clean sweep of the Outer Drive and its six lanes of hurtling traffic, and the iron-gray background of the lake spreading and merging indistinguishably into the somber horizon. He watched the microscopic movement of people hurrying along the sidewalks, massing momentarily at stop lights like ants meeting an unexpected obstacle, and then spilling onward again when the signals changed.

Jake sighed and went back to his desk. He worked for a few hours, accomplishing little. He was glad when his phone rang. It was Noble.

"Jake, get down to my office right away. Damn it, all hell has broken loose."

The crisis tone was in his voice.

Jake said okay.

CHAPTER FIVE

N<small>OBLE</small> was pacing up and down before his desk when Jake walked in, and the expression on his normally beaming face would have fitted a man whose brokers had sold him short on the same day his wife had run off with a best friend. When he saw Jake he threw up his hands in dramatic despair.

"We've been had, Jake," he said hoarsely. "Look." He grabbed a paper from his desk and pointed a trembling forefinger at a story that ran about sixty per cent of column one on the front page.

There was a picture and an account of May's murder on the same page, but Noble was referring to another story, one which had been given to the papers by Gregory Prior.

Jake sat on the edge of Noble's desk and ran quickly down through the column. Prior had explained that his job was to investigate certain of Mr. Dan Riordan's wartime contracts, and to pass on his findings to the Senatorial committee. That much was okay.

The lead pipe descended in the last paragraph.

There Prior was quoted as saying:

". . . Mr. Riordan's high-powered press representatives have already sought me out, and have attempted to present their client to me as a man who did no worse than many others. Naturally, I do not intend to be influenced by these paid apologists. . . ."

There was more, but Jake tossed the paper down, and said, "Well, I'll be damned."

"Where did he get that story?" Noble said desperately.

"From me," Jake said. "I met Prior at May's this morning, and tried to creep into his heart. My charms are fading, I guess."

"What the hell are we going to do?"

"I'll tell you what," Jake said. "I'm going to make that well-scrubbed bastard regret that he ever came near Chicago. The first thing I'll do—"

Noble's phone interrupted him. Noble picked up the receiver, and flashed a glance at Jake. "Yes, Mr. Riordan, we've seen it," he said.

Jake saw the perspiration beading Noble's forehead. "That story was a mistake," Noble said, with a wave at Jake. "All a mistake. You see . . ."

Jake took the phone from Noble's hand. "This is Jake Harrison, Mr. Riordan. I was responsible for that story."

Riordan's voice was harsh. "Well, damn it, were you out of your head, or just drunk?"

"Let's relax a little," Jake said. "I met Prior this morning at May Laval's and took a chance on getting him into a cooperative mood with a show of frankness. I told him I was speaking off the record, which, as you probably know, is a convention that people in this business respect. Prior doesn't, obviously."

"Well, what are we going to do? That story makes me look like a crook who's hired a lot of fast-talking press agents because he's scared of the truth coming out."

"We'll take care of that. This afternoon we'll have a press conference. How's three o'clock for you?"

"The time is all right, but what will I say?"

"Leave that to me. I'll set this up at three in your suite, and we'll be over around two for a rehearsal. You've heard about May Laval, I suppose?"

"Yes, I read the papers. I—damn shame, I suppose. I spent last night in Gary and got the news when I got back to town. Did you see Avery Meed?"

"Yes, he just left."

"I see." Riordan sounded relieved. "I'm waiting for him, but he should be along pretty soon, I suppose."

"I suppose," Jake said, and dropped the receiver back in place.

Noble was at the bar making himself a drink. He brought it to the desk and sat down nervously. "A press conference this afternoon is rushing things a little," he said. "The boys from the papers can make him look pretty bad."

Jake shrugged. "We've got no choice. The longer we wait after this blast of Prior's the weaker our case gets. You'd better have your secretary call the papers and the wire services and tell them about the conference. I'll get Niccolo to work on Riordan's handout."

"Let's talk about that a minute," Noble said, rubbing his forehead gloomily. "What the hell *can* he say?"

"I think we'd better play it safe. We'll hammer away at the point that so far the government has made no specific accusations, but is high-handedly damning Riordan in the press. We'll make Riordan the baffled, injured victim of fascist bureaucracy. I know it's not a brilliant pitch, but it's worked before." Jake lit a cigarette and tossed the match away irritably. "I'm not in a genius mood. All my ideas run toward putting a midget on Riordan's lap. Also, I hope to hell he can prove he spent the night in Gary. That will at least eliminate him as a candidate for the electric chair."

"I see what you mean," Noble said, and stared at his drink with a solemn expression.

Jake tried unsuccessfully to find Niccolo; but Dean had apparently gone out for a mid-morning snack. He returned to his office, rolled a clean sheet of paper into his typewriter and knocked out the speech for Riordan in half an hour. He had coffee and a sandwich at his desk, and rewrote the speech once more, trying to strike a tone that would sound unrehearsed and extemporaneous when Riordan reeled it off for the press.

Lieutenant Martin called him at one o'clock.

"Anything new?" Jake said.

"Nothing interesting," Martin said. He sounded dour. "We've checked the obvious things. May had two servants, a maid and cleaning woman, but neither of them slept there. The cleaning woman came in at six in the morning, because May frequently had breakfast parties around ten or eleven."

"They call it brunch," Jake said.

"Yeah, they would. Anyway, the maid left at two this morning. The party was over then, but one guy was hanging around. Guy named Rengale. I talked with him, and he says he left about two fifteen. Do you know him?"

"Yes," Jake said.

"Damn idiot," Martin said. "Talked my arm off about soap operas. He says they're the tone poems of the people, whatever the hell that means. Anyway, he's clear. He was at a bar in the loop from a quarter of three to six thirty."

"You didn't find the diary, I presume."

"No. But I want to talk to your boy, Riordan."

"I'm afraid that's a blind alley. He spent the night in Gary."

"Yeah? What was he doing in Gary?"

"Damn it, how should I know? He owns steel mills in Gary. Maybe he went out to puddle some steel, or whatever it is you do with steel. When are you going to see him?"

"I thought you'd like to suggest a time."

"That's decent of you, my friend. Could you make it around four thirty? We're having a press conference at three, and it would louse up our pitch if you arrived to arrest him about that time."

"I'm not going to arrest him. Four thirty will be fine."

"Thanks. Let me know if I can ever fix a parking ticket for you."

"I fix my own," Martin said. He paused, then said in a determined but embarrassed voice, "There is a little thing, Jake. My kid is having a birthday party this afternoon, and the wife thought it would be nice if he got his picture in the paper. Along with all the other kids, of course," he added hastily. "I promised her I'd talk to somebody. You know how women are, Jake, they go nuts every time their kids get a new tooth or learn a new word."

"Why, of course," Jake said. "But you fathers are different. You don't pay any attention to your children, unless they do something impressive, such as throwing a handful of strained spinach against the wall."

"Oh, cut it out. Do you think it can be arranged?"

"Sure," Jake said. "And thanks again for holding off

on Riordan."

"Okay," Martin said.

Jake called the city desk of the *Tribune*. He asked Mike Hanlon, an old friend, if they had a photographer to spare for a kid's birthday party. Mike said sure, that everybody liked pictures of kids. And dogs, he added.

Jake put Riordan's speech in his pocket and started to look for Noble. He stopped at the open door of Sheila's office. She had her feet on her desk and was studying a huge cardboard sheet propped against the wall. The cardboard was covered with clips from various papers, and the inscriptions above them told anyone who cared that they represented editorial space that had used items about that prince of crackers, Toastee Cracker.

Jake walked in and sat on the edge of her desk.

"Admiring the kill?" he said, and patted her slim ankles.

Sheila put her feet on the floor. "You lost your extra-territorial rights, remember?"

Jake snapped his fingers. "I keep forgetting. Don't you think there's something unnatural about our working in such proximity?"

"I don't feel unnatural," Sheila said. "But I find your absent-minded passes a little disturbing. What do you think of that?" she said, nodding toward the

Toastee Cracker display. "I got cracker recipes in two hundred cooking columns and had it plugged on the air about five hundred times on hints-for-the-home program. Not bad, eh?"

"No, in fact it's damn good. Gary see this?"

"Yes, about fifteen minutes ago, but he's too upset to care. He gave it a startled look and said, 'Grand! Grand!' before rushing off. What's on his mind?"

"The Riordan press conference," Jake said.

"You wrote Riordan's speech, I suppose. Did you make him sound like Nathan Hale?"

"Stop being disdainful. I can't stand any of your idealistic contempt right now. How about coming over to Riordan's with us?"

Sheila glanced at her watch and frowned. "I've got to get six releases into the mails by four. You can't begin to loathe crackers until you've considered all the horrible things you can do with them. I've stuffed crackers into everything but the food editors' mouths."

"Have you tried soaking them overnight in a saucer of bonded Sterno? Serves four and serves them right. Come on."

"Okay," Sheila said. She smiled and got to her feet. "Gary won't mind, will he?"

"He won't be conscious. Hurry."

Jake walked on to Noble's office feeling better. Sheila would be an asset. She knew how to mix drinks and talk shop with the press.

Niccolo was coming through the reception room when Jake reached there. "I heard you wanted me this morning, Jake. Anything important?"

"Riordan's handout for the press conference," Jake said. "I did it myself. You'd better come on with us now. I'll want you to do some releases later this week, and you can get some background this afternoon."

"Okay."

Jake went into Noble's office without knocking. Noble had shaved and changed into another suit and his thick white hair had been disarranged with the usual care.

"Let's go," Jake said.

They met Niccolo and Sheila in the reception room and walked out to the elevators and, for some reason, no one was very cheerful.

"Well, buck up," Noble said, smiling nervously. "We've done it before and we can do it again."

"Blacken your faces, men, we're going in," Niccolo said, solemnly, and winked at Jake.

CHAPTER SIX

THEY arrived at Riordan's suite in the Blackstone Hotel at two o'clock. The door was opened by Riordan's wife, Denise, who had a highball glass in one hand.

"Come on in," she said. "Danny is dressing, but he won't be long."

Brian Riordan was slumped in a deep chair by the fireplace, with one leg hooked over its arm and a drink in his hand. He was wearing Bry tweeds and a few strands of his sandy hair were falling over his forehead.

"Here come the white knights to the old man's rescue," he said grinning. "Have you got a de luxe halo to clap on his head, and an orchestra to play celestial music in the background?"

Denise said, "Oh, stop it, Brian."

Noble handled the introductions. Brian nodded absently at Sheila and said to Niccolo, "Haven't we met before?"

Niccolo said, "Yes. You were waiting for an elevator

the other night at the office when I got off. You were concerned about whether or not I'd been in the army."

"Well, I was a little drunk," Brian said. "But it's a good question. Were you?"

"It's a silly question," Denise said. "Can't I fix you people something to drink?"

Sheila sat down on the divan and gave Jake a quick amused glance. "Yes, I'll have a scotch and soda since everything is so clubby."

Brian grinned at her. "Don't knock yourself out being sarcastic. I'm inconsiderate as hell, I know. I'm eternally curious about what other people did while I was dropping little messages of good cheer on the Germans. Some of them did the funniest things. My father, for instance. He made money. And how about yourself? Did you have a nice war?"

"I wasn't in the paratroops, if that's what you mean," Sheila said. "But I didn't have a nice war."

The bedroom door opened and Dan Riordan walked in, freshly shaven and wearing a double breasted gray flannel suit.

He walked restlessly to the window, pulled back the drapes, then dropped them and returned to the center of the room.

"Any details about May's murder?" he asked, of no one in particular.

There was an odd silence in the room and Jake had the impression that Riordan had mentioned the thought that was on everyone's mind.

"I just have the bare facts," Noble said.

Jake settled back in his chair and glanced around. Brian Riordan was blowing smoke rings into the air, and Denise had crossed her legs and was fingering the arm of her chair distractedly. Sheila was watching Riordan, who was frowning at Noble, as if he'd said something significant.

Practically everybody present, Jake realized, was probably relieved that May had been murdered. Riordan, certainly. And Denise and Brian, also, since it secured the health and productivity of their golden goose. Sheila had no reason to care, but Noble was undoubtedly happy that an obstacle in the way of the account had been removed.

The question was, had any of these people killed May?

Riordan, who had the best reason to murder May, had spent the night in Gary, Indiana. Noble had no alibi, other than his own word that he'd spent the night with one Bebe Passione. Jake wondered where Denise Riordan had been last night, since no one had mentioned her being in Gary with her husband. And Brian. Where had he been?

Riordan put a cigar in his mouth and lit it with a silver lighter from the coffee table.

"The police have any ideas yet?" he said.

"Not so far," Jake said. "She was killed around four,

strangled with a sash from her negligee. They know that her diary is missing. And," he paused, and glanced at Riordan, "they know the diary is presumed to have some hot information about you."

"How do they know that?" Riordan said quietly.

"I told them."

"Any reason for that?"

"Yes, of course. You and May had an argument about her plans for the book, which was overheard by most of the people at her party. The police would learn about that, so I told them to make it appear we, or you, rather, have nothing to fear."

"I have nothing to fear," Riordan said. "Your assumption that I need to be defended is a little odd, Harrison."

Jake sighed. "It's an occupational disease with me to copper all bets. I'm glad you have nothing to fear, because you have an appointment with Lieutenant Martin of the Homicide Division at four thirty this afternoon."

"How do you know that?"

"He asked me when it would be convenient for him to see you. I suggested he make it after the press conference. For obvious reasons."

"I see." Riordan frowned and then began to nod thoughtfully. "You mean, Martin is willing to cooperate because you were square with him about me. You were right." He grinned suddenly. "You're doing fine, Harrison."

Denise stood up impatiently. "I hate all of this," she said. "May Laval was a flamboyant bitch, and she couldn't even die without making a scene. People will be saying you killed her to get the diary, Danny."

"People will say no such thing," Riordan said icily. He stared at his wife with controlled but unmistakable anger. "I was in Gary last night, if you remember."

Brian Riordan suddenly clapped his hands together in applause. "Tycoon saved by last minute alibi," he intoned. "Free Enterprise wins again."

"Oh, shut up," his father said.

"That's the trouble with all you people, you're so deadly serious," Brian said, getting languidly to his feet. "Come, Denise, I'll take you as far as the elevator."

Denise kissed Riordan on the cheek and picked up an alligator bag that matched her pumps, and a seven-skin sable which provided the last exquisitely expensive touch to her appearance. "I'm going to do some shopping," she said, and smiled around the room. "See you all again soon, I hope."

Jake wondered if she had told Riordan about her visit to May's. The police would get to that eventually, and so would the papers. They couldn't do much, however, unless Denise or Brian was foolish enough to disclose their intention of buying or scaring her out of writing her book.

Brian waved to Niccolo from the doorway. "Don't take any wooden foxholes, chum."

Denise plucked at his arm. "Let's don't get into the Battle of the Bulge with sound effects here."

They left, closing the door behind them. Jake stood up and took the speech he'd written from his breast pocket, and handed it to Riordan. "Look it over and we'll talk about it a bit."

While Riordan read the speech Jake found his thoughts turning back to May. He couldn't get her from his mind. There was that business she'd had with Mike Francesca, the aging but still potent racketeer. Jake wondered if Martin had a line on Francesca yet.

"It doesn't cover much ground," Riordan said, jerking Jake back to the present.

"There's not much ground we can cover safely," Jake said. "That speech will be okay if you handle it right. Read it again, then throw it away. Don't bother trying to memorize it, but get the ideas across in your own words. You're making just one point today, namely, that no formal charges have been brought against you, that you're in the dark, and at the mercy of the government until such a time as they stop trying your case in the newspapers and charge you specifically with something—even if it's only playing your radio too loudly."

"I get your idea now," Riordan said.

"Fine. When you start talking, preface your remarks

by stating that you'll answer all questions when you're through. There may be some embarrassing ones, but don't say 'No comment' to anything. If you don't want to answer a question, say you can't do it at this time, or that you don't know." He glanced at his watch. "Remember, these guys can spot a phony act a mile away, so just relax and be natural. Now, I'd suggest that you wait in the bedroom until they get here. Do you have anything to add, Gary?"

"One other thing," Noble said hastily. "The liquor."

Riordan waved to the phone. "Room service will send you anything you need," he said and left.

Niccolo slumped down in the chair that Brian had vacated. "Did you ever hear a sillier idiot than young Riordan?" he said.

"Maladjusted, mayhaps," Sheila said.

"He's making a cult out of it," Niccolo said disgustedly. He glanced at his watch nervously. "What the hell is holding up the press?"

"They're in no hurry to get their ears bent," Jake said. "They're probably all sensibly having a beer somewhere."

Ten minutes after the waiters had brought in trays of whiskey and soda there was a knock on the door and Noble squared his shoulders, drew his face into a broad welcoming smile and marched across the room with the springy gait of a Rotary chairman on stunt night.

Fifteen minutes later the room was crowded with photographers and reporters. Jake saw that the release on Riordan's speech was distributed to everyone, and that the drinks flowed smoothly. He had known many of the reporters for years and he talked with them easily, and almost automatically got across the pitch he hoped they would take back to their editors.

He made the point, unobtrusively, that Riordan was in the dark because Prior, the bastard from the government, was making him out to be a crook in advance of any charges or evidence. That was as far as Jake cared to go, since he knew that most of the men covering the story didn't give much of a damn about it, merely wanted to get it over with, get it written and off their minds.

Jake, himself, wasn't too interested in selling them one way or the other, and this puzzled him. Normally, he thought, it could at least be said of him that he worked and fought hard for a client. That didn't seem to be true now. He decided the trouble was May. Until he knew what had happened to her and why he wouldn't be good for much else. Why that should be so he didn't know.

Noble called for attention and after the buzz of talk died he smiled gratefully, and opened the bedroom door. "All set, Mr. Riordan," he said.

Riordan came out immediately and shook hands all around, and said hello to several of the reporters he'd known during the war. The photographers wanted to get their shots and clear out, so he posed for them and then waved the reporters into chairs and got into his speech.

He was good at handling men. He stood in the center of the room and something in his manner made that the only natural place for him to stand. He stumbled for words occasionally, but he made his points with strong emphasis, and he came through as an angry but baffled man who wanted only to be told what the shouting was about so he could say a word in his own defense.

Afterward, when the reporters had left and Noble had distributed drinks jubilantly, Jake sat down beside Sheila. Noble was telling Riordan how well he'd done, and Riordan was puffing a cigar and smiling cheerfully.

"Well, how did we do?" Jake said to Sheila.

"Oh, fine. I'll tell you about it some time."

"I know what you're thinking," Jake said. He felt an unaccountable depression. "Does your offer to help me get drunk still stand?"

"If you like."

Riordan was almost jubilant, Jake noticed. When the phone rang, he said, "I'll bet this is Meed," and scooped up the receiver with a strong quick gesture. "Riordan speaking," he said.

He listened a moment and then he spoke and his

voice was low and hard. "I'll be right over," he said.

He lowered his hand to his side, still holding the receiver, and stared straight ahead with a curiously disbelieving expression on his face.

"What is it?" Noble said anxiously.

Riordan put a hand to his forehead and shook his head slowly. "Avery Meed was murdered in his hotel room this morning. I—that was a Lieutenant Martin on the phone. He wants me to come over there now."

He took a step forward and noticed that he was still holding the phone. Frowning at it, he let it drop to the floor. He walked to the coffee table and poured himself a drink.

Sheila had sat up straight, and Noble was breathing heavily, obviously torn between the desire to say something, and the knowledge that there wasn't anything to say.

Niccolo alone seemed calm. He picked the phone from the floor and replaced it in the cradle. "You'd better take a cab if they want you in a hurry," he said to Riordan.

"Yes, yes," Riordan said, putting his drink down. "Call the bell captain. I'll be ready to go in a few minutes."

He walked into the bedroom and Noble stared at Jake with shoulders expressively raised. "What the hell does this mean?" he said.

"Who knows?" Jake said. "Somebody's killed Meed,

I gather. I'll go with Riordan and find out what I can."

"Fine," Noble said. He seemed relieved that some-one was taking action which, whether effective or not, relieved him of the responsibility of doing anything.

When Riordan came out of the bedroom wearing a hat and topcoat, Jake jumped up and followed him through the door.

CHAPTER SEVEN

Avery Meed had lived in a quiet residential hotel on the South Side, about twenty minutes' drive from the Loop. Riordan explained to Jake on the way out that Meed had maintained the apartment in Chicago, and a place in Washington which he had used when business took him to the capital. Meed had never married and, so far as Riordan knew, had no outside interests.

The hotel lobby was quiet and chaste, with somber green carpeting and straight-backed chairs placed in regular formation against the gray walls. An elderly clerk stood at the reception desk, and behind him were racks of pigeonholes for mail. The only incongruous note in the atmosphere of determined dullness was the presence of the uniformed policeman at the elevators.

Jake told him who they were and he waved them into a car. Lieutenant Martin met them at the door of Meed's apartment, looking, Jake noticed, tired and stubborn and angry.

"You're Riordan, I suppose," he said. "Come on in." To Jake he said, "What brings you here?"

"I was at Mr. Riordan's when you called, so I came along. Am I in the way?"

"No, stick around. You got any idea who might have killed Meed, Riordan?"

Riordan hesitated, as if giving the matter careful thought. Then he shook his head. "No, I haven't."

"Come on into the bedroom," Martin said.

They followed him into the bedroom where two lab men were checking for fingerprints. The one off-key note in the spare, ascetic room was the body that lay on the bed, staring sightlessly at the calcimined ceiling.

Meed had been strangled to death with one of his own soberly correct neckties. He had died painfully and messily.

After what seemed a very long time Martin said, "We can talk in the living room," and led the way back. He closed the bedroom door and nodded to Riordan. "You have anything to suggest?" he asked.

Riordan hesitated, and then said, "Yes," in a quiet, firm voice.

"Let's have it," Martin said.

Riordan sat down in an overstuffed chair by the window, deliberately unwrapped a cigar and lighted it; when it was drawing well he said, "This morning, at my orders, Avery Meed went to May Laval's home to get her diary. That's news to you, I'm sure, Lieutenant."

Martin's normally pleasant face took on a hard, unfriendly expression. "Yeah, that's news," he said. "Supposing you go right on surprising me, Riordan."

Riordan appeared unimpressed by Martin's tone and manner.

"First, let me give you some background," he said. "I knew May Laval during the war. Knew her quite well, as a matter of fact. May's home was a gathering place for important people then and I spent a good deal of time there. May, it has developed recently, kept a diary during those years, which she intended to publish in the form of an exposé."

"There's material about you in the diary that wouldn't look good in print, I suppose," Martin said.

"That's right," Riordan said calmly. "And Lieutenant, remember this: No one can make the money I have without also cutting corners and making enemies. I'm having trouble right now with a Congressional investigation, and this book of May's could have been very embarrassing. So last night I told Avery Meed to go to her home and get the diary."

"What time was this?"

"That I told him? About twelve thirty last night I called him. I told him to meet any price she wanted, but to be damn sure he got all references from her diary that related to me."

"That was twelve thirty, eh?" Martin said. "Where did you spend the night, Riordan?"

"In Gary. I had some production bugs to iron out with my plant manager there, so I went out and spent the night with him."

"What's your manager's name?"

"Devlin. Robert Devlin. You want to check with him that I'm not lying?"

"Go on with your story," Martin said.

Riordan smiled slightly. "Okay. This morning at seven o'clock Meed called me in Gary. He said he had the diary. He also had something important to discuss with me, but he wouldn't talk on the phone. He had an appointment with Mr. Harrison here at nine, so I told him to keep that, and then meet me at my hotel at eleven."

"He didn't show up, of course," Martin said.

"No."

Martin glanced at Jake. "Then you saw Meed this morning?"

"Yes, at nine thirty. We talked until ten. That's about all I can give you."

"Did he seem upset?"

"He wasn't that sort."

Martin said, "Riordan, do you think Meed murdered May Laval to get the diary?"

Riordan knocked ash from his cigar and shrugged. "Who knows?" he said. "I told him to get the diary.

Meed was the kind of person who did what he was told. Maybe May wouldn't go for the cash settlement. Meed's reaction to that obstacle would have been interesting. Picture him, the perfect automaton, moving ahead under orders from on high. Suddenly, the way is blocked." Riordan paused and glanced at Jake expressively. "You met Meed, Harrison. What do you think he would have done?"

"No comment," Jake said drily.

"You think he would have killed her to get the diary?" Martin said, slowly.

"I honestly don't know," Riordan said.

There was a silence in the room for a few seconds, while Martin rubbed his jaw and stared moodily out the windows. Finally he shrugged, and said, "Here's what we know for sure. Meed came in here this morning at about six o'clock. Later, around a quarter of nine, he left, presumably to keep his appointment with you, Jake. He got back here at approximately ten fifteen. He received a call from someone at ten thirty-five, which he answered. Later in the day he got two more calls, which he didn't answer. Around two thirty the cleaning woman entered his room and found him lying on the bed just as he is now. She called the desk. They called us."

"I called him here twice this afternoon," Riordan said.

"He was dead then. The coroner put the time of

death between ten thirty and eleven thirty." Martin lit a cigarette carefully and studied Riordan. "Now we get to the big question: Where's the diary now?"

"You didn't find it here?" Riordan asked thoughtfully.

"We've been through this place pretty thoroughly. We didn't find anything that looked like May's diary. You got any ideas where it might be?"

"No, I haven't," Riordan said, in the same thoughtful voice. He drew slowly on his cigar, then crushed it out in the ash tray with a slow, deliberate gesture. The cigar broke under the pressure. Riordan continued to press downward until the last spark died, the last wisp of smoke disappeared. Then he said, quietly, "Meed got the diary. Somebody killed him and took the diary. That's the person I want to find."

"We have an interest in that, too," Martin said.

Riordan stood and picked up his hat. "You may get him before I do," he said. "I don't know. But remember this: I was ready to pay nearly anything for that diary. I'm not going to be stopped now. Frankly, I don't give much of a damn that Meed was murdered. To me, he was a well-oiled, smoothly-functioning cog that never gave any trouble. He's no use to me now. But I want the diary."

"Sure you do," Martin said, with a humorless smile. "The dirt on you is now in somebody else's hands, isn't it?"

"That was my first thought when you called me," Riordan said. "Now, if you don't need me any more, I'll run along."

"Sure," Martin said.

Jake said goodbye and left with Riordan. Downstairs Riordan shook hands with him, and then caught a cab to his hotel. Jake hailed the next one and rode back downtown to the office. There were a number of stray thoughts in his mind, but he couldn't work up enough enthusiasm to fit them into a pattern. He felt tired for no reason at all, and vaguely depressed.

Sheila was typing with a concentrated frown on her face when he walked into her office. She stopped and pulled the paper from her typewriter.

"Ready for our bacchanalian binge?" he said.

"It's only four thirty, Jake."

"So?"

"Okay. But what about Meed?"

"I'll tell you later."

Jake watched her as she touched up her lipstick, and smoothed her dark hair quickly and unnecessarily. She went to the wall mirror and he noticed the unconscious grace of her movements as she adjusted her small green hat. He sighed and looked out the window.

Fog had been rolling in from the lake, and the streets below were hidden in layers of swirling grayness; the towers of the Loop rested on this fog-cloud like the minarets of a ghost city.

Sheila came to his side and put her hand on his arm. "Depressing, isn't it? Looks like one strong wind could blow it all away."

"Yes, it does," Jake said. "And in about five more seconds I'm likely to say something esoteric and mystical. So let's get the hell out of here."

They had cocktails and dinner at the Palmer House, and finally wound up at Dave's on Michigan Boulevard. Jake lit a cigarette and tried to relax. Dave's was good for that; the décor was stubbornly and restfully old-fashioned. There was a small circular bar, happily free from fancy bottle displays, neon lighting, drink-a-birds, and chromium popcorn bowls; there were also spacious wooden booths in the back, where conversation could flourish without the hamstringing influence of jukeboxes or television.

Dave's was within three minutes' walk from the offices of Mutual and Columbia, and was a haven for weary writers and radio directors who liked to drink in an atmosphere that didn't remind them of the lacquered hysteria of their jobs. Now, Jake saw there were two stand-by announcers from CBS at the bar, having a quick one between station breaks, and two tired copy-writers sat at the opposite rim of the bar, discussing without any genuine interest the relative merits of advertising and tuck-pointing as professions.

Sheila sipped her brandy. "Well, let's get drunk."

"Oh, great," Jake said.

Sheila put her feet up on the opposite seat and crossed her ankles comfortably. "What's wrong with you? No epigrams, no impish revelry. You make me a little sad."

Jake sipped his drink. "That's quite an indictment. What do you suggest?"

"I'd suggest you call Gary Noble right now and tell him you're turning in your typewriter and hand-painted tie for good. Then find yourself an honest job. Maybe you'd make a good sharecropper. But naturally you won't do that."

"Naturally," Jake said. "But why do you think it would help?"

"I think you're getting fed up with yourself, Jake. I think you're getting an oh-so-tiny pang of conscience about the Riordan account."

"Oh, stop it," Jake said irritably. "Why should I have pangs of conscience about the Riordan account? It's just a job."

"Supposing he's proved to be a war profiteer? Would that make any difference in your thinking?"

"I would suggest to Gary that we double our fee, that's all. Sheila, honey, I'm not sincere or idealistic. Now let's talk about something cheerful."

"Okay. What do you want to talk about?"

"I don't want to talk about May, but she's on my

107

mind. This afternoon I learned that Riordan sent his prim little hatchet man, Avery Meed, to get the diary from her. Meed apparently succeeded. But then somebody killed him. The diary is again missing."

"What are the details?"

Jake told her what he knew. When he finished Sheila made a little circle with the bottom of her glass on the table. For a moment she was silent. Then she said, "What does Martin think?"

"He seems to be in the dark. But I wouldn't like to be the boy he's after."

"You look harried enough to fit the role. Jake, this may be a far-fetched idea, but could Riordan have killed Meed?"

Jake looked at her sharply. "What do you mean?"

"Supposing Meed murdered May and got the diary. And supposing Meed suddenly decided then that he could blackmail Riordan very profitably. That's a possibility, at least. Riordan might have had to kill him to get the diary. He has no alibi for the time Meed was killed, remember."

"That's right," Jake said. Then he shrugged. "But I can't let you hang a murder rap on my client. If Riordan's a murderer I don't want it to get bruited about."

"Naturally," Sheila said drily. She sipped her drink, and said, "Mind if I ask you a personal question, Jake?"

"Why, no. Go ahead."

"Maybe I should know the answer, having shared your bed and board for two years. But just what do you believe in?"

Jake waved to Dave for another round. "We're going to be here a long time," he said. "I don't know why it is, dear, but that question always makes people excited and garrulous. They will worry it around all night until someone gets glassy-eyed and belligerent because he can't convince everyone else that the only thing to believe in is sex rampant or the dictatorship of the proletariat."

"Oh, stop being so utterly, utterly clever," Sheila said. "I asked you a serious question. Do you want to answer it or not?"

"Okay, I'll try," Jake said resignedly. "Dear, a man can believe in anything at all if he tries hard enough and gets some satisfaction out of it. The world is full of apothegms, slogans, religious proverbs and old saws, that are more or less true, and which can be adapted to any temperament and situation. There are a thousand to choose from, and they're all shining and beautiful. Honesty is the best policy! Hamilton is a fine watch! Every cloud must have a silver lining! It's the rich what gets the pleasure! Take your pick. They're all wonderful, I believe in them all, though I've lately been toying with the heretical notion that possibly there may be other watches almost as fine as Hamilton."

"Let's forget I asked," Sheila said. "That mood of brittle elfishness you affect is quite a bore. I gather though that Riordan's innocence or guilt doesn't make any difference to you?"

"Well, why should it? I'm not his confessor."

"How long are you going to kid yourself? Eventually, Jake, you're going to wind up with Noble's attitude, that a dollar is its own reward, and that decency is a droll superstition for peasants."

"Oh, it's not that bad," Jake said. He felt uncomfortable. He didn't enjoy self-examination. "Supposing Riordan's guilty? I don't see that it's my concern. As a press agent I'm retained to make him look good. Hell, we'll create a bumper demand for lousy barrels, and Riordan can corner the market in the next war."

Sheila looked at him for a moment in silence; then she picked up her purse and gloves and slid from the booth.

"I'm going to run along."

"Oh, don't go off in a pout," Jake said. "I know you're disgusted. I am, too. My mother must have been scared by a corny gag before I was born. Don't leave me tonight, Sheila."

"Sorry, Jake. You're just not very funny."

He watched her walk through the bar, and let herself out the door. Sighing, he picked up his drink. . . .

Two hours later Dave came back and sat down in the opposite seat, his homely face sympathetic.

"What's the matter?"

Jake finished his drink. "I'm not funny, Dave," he said.

"Ah, who says that?"

"Sheila. She told me in a simple declarative sentence that I am not funny."

"Ah, women," Dave said. "They got no sense of humor. They laugh because they seen men doing it. But take it easy on the booze, Jake. You can't drink it all yourself."

"Don't worry. I'm running along."

Dave came with him to the door, and helped him into his topcoat.

"She was right, of course," Jake said.

"Yeah, sure."

"I'm very unfunny," Jake said, and went out the door.

He lay awake that night for what seemed a long time. The liquor wore away slowly, leaving him tired and depressed. Why did he always behave like such a sophomoric idiot with Sheila? Why did he delight in trying to shock her, like some nasty little boy scribbling four-letter words where the nice little girl across the street would be sure to see them? Lighting another cigarette, he tried to get his mind on something else. The only alternative was the murders of May and Avery Meed, and thinking of them led him to a frustrating dead end. There was nothing in either death that could be checked on, investigated or speculated about. May had been murdered. Avery Meed had been murdered. And so far there was nothing but these brute facts to consider.

But as he put out the cigarette a few minutes later, he remembered something. Noble had told him he'd spent the night with Bebe Passione at the Regis; he had wanted Jake to cover up for the sake of his wife.

Thinking about Noble's story, Jake began to wonder whether it wasn't too pat and plausible. Anyone knowing Noble would immediately believe it, of course. Noble was born to be involved with a chorus girl on the night of a murder for which he would need an alibi. But if Noble was lying, he had been at least smart enough to type-cast himself in a preposterous, and hence believable, situation.

Jake grinned and picked up his phone. He asked the club operator to get him the Regis Hotel.

He talked to the hotel clerk very briefly. And when he put the phone slowly back into its cradle he was no longer smiling.

Bebe Passione had left for Miami ten days ago.

CHAPTER EIGHT

J ake got down to work the next morning at ten thirty and found Noble in his office exulting over the morning papers.

"Did you see these, Jake?" he cried happily. "They're beautiful, simply beautiful."

Jake hadn't. He walked around behind Noble's desk and glanced at the stories, which had been inspired by the press conference in Riordan's suite the previous afternoon.

From the agency's and Riordan's standpoint, they were excellent. The dominant tone was that Riordan was being harried by officious government snoops. There was, in addition to the straight news coverage, a feature story on Riordan's Chicago plants in the *News*, with production figures to indicate their importance to the war effort. And in a front page editorial entitled STOP THE WITCH HUNT, the *Tribune* ominously warned its readership that free enterprise and the American Dream were being threatened by these promiscuous and irresponsible investigations.

The editorial made the point that the Hampstead Committee was not a specially privileged unit, and should not take unto itself the authoritarian powers of a police state. The Committee, the editorial concluded, under the direction of one Gregory Prior, had brought no charges against Mr. Riordan, but had, nevertheless, already damaged his reputation by implication and innuendo.

"Get that line about Gregory Prior," Noble said, delightedly. "Jake, we're off to a running start."

"Did we make the wires on any of this stuff?" Jake asked.

"You're damned right. AP and UP covered, and *Time* has already called this morning and asked for dope on Riordan. I got Niccolo busy on a handout."

"Fine," Jake said.

He picked up a fresh copy of the *Tribune* from Noble's desk and took it to the bar, while Noble began to outline an idea for a picture story on Riordan's family life, with the accent to be laid heavily on its domestic simplicity and young Brian's war record.

Jake listened absently and went through the paper. The murder of Avery Meed was on the first page, the fact of his having been Riordan's secretary giving it additional news value. May was on page four now, and there were no further developments in either case. The police were investigating several possibilities and were expecting a conclusive development within the next twenty-four hours. Jake wondered why they always said just that; and wondered what would happen if they announced instead that they had lost all interest in the case and were now engrossed with making ceramics.

Noble suddenly pounded his fist on the desk, and said, "There! What do you think of that?"

"Oh, great," Jake said. "I'll get someone on it right away."

"Jake, you act like you're tired or something."

"I was taken unexpectedly drunk last night," Jake said, and winced. He wondered if he were likely to develop into the sort of graceless idiot who was never at a loss for rakish comments about his hangovers.

Mixing a drink, he caught sight of himself in the mirror behind the bar. He was wearing a dark gray suit, with a neatly knotted blue silk tie. His graying hair was combed down smoothly and he was freshly shaved. But his face was pale and drawn, and his eyes were tired. He looked like a man of distinction who had gone hog-wild over the sponsor's product.

Noble watched him in the mirror. "You'd better check into a steam bath this afternoon," he said. "We've got to be at top form from now on, you know."

"Yes, I know," Jake said. He sipped his drink and met Noble's eyes in the mirror. "Where were you the night that May was killed, Gary?"

Noble remained motionless behind his desk, staring

115

at Jake expressionlessly; but Jake saw his hand move and close nervously on the handle of a long letter opener.

"Why do you want to know?" he said finally.

Jake turned from the bar and shrugged. "Let's don't make small talk. I found out last night that Bebe Passione hadn't been in town for ten days. She's in Miami. You said you were with her the night before last when May was killed. I know damn well you weren't in Miami, Gary. So where were you?"

"I went to see May that night," Noble said, and suddenly he looked old and frightened. The color left his normally ruddy cheeks, and he ran both hands nervously through his rumpled white hair. He met Jake's eyes anxiously. "I—I thought I could clear up that business about the diary. Jake, I need the Riordan account. Grant's cancelled last week, but I didn't tell anybody about it, not even you. You know I can't talk about a lost account. It's like talking about dying. Anyway, I thought if I could straighten things out with May it would put us in solidly with Riordan."

Jake sat down tiredly in a deep leather chair and rested his head against the back. "Was she alive?" he asked.

"Yes, she was alive," Noble said quickly. "I got there around two thirty, I guess. I told her what I wanted, but she wouldn't go for it, Jake. She didn't want money."

"What did she want?" Jake asked.

Noble shrugged helplessly. "I don't know what she wanted, Jake. She seemed glad to see me, and we had a drink or two. But I couldn't make any progress with her. She was just in one of those moods. She said she was expecting someone else at three and hustled me out."

"Yes? That's interesting. Who?"

"She didn't say." Noble scratched his head. "But it was odd. She told me about it, and then she laughed. It was a private joke, I gathered."

"Okay. You said she was in 'one of those moods.' What do you mean?"

"I'll be damned if I know exactly," Noble said, frowning. "But it was just that she didn't seem to be taking me or herself seriously. It was all an act we might have been doing in a charade game. There was a young ass from Chicago University there when I arrived. Maybe she was showing off for him. He had a crew cut and horn-rimmed glasses and was behaving as if he'd been on a steady diet of Oscar Wilde for years."

"This was two thirty?"

"Yes, and May was wearing red silk Mandarin pajamas and there was incense burning on the mantle." Noble shook his head. "It was all pretty disgusting."

"That's a fine middle-class attitude," Jake said. "What you mean is that her refusal to be bribed by you was disgusting."

"Don't snap at me," Noble said, peevishly. "I'm not up to it. Maybe 'picturesque' is what I meant. At any rate she chased this character from the University, and we got down to business. But we didn't get down far enough. She just laughed at me, said she was touched by my concern for Riordan, but that she couldn't let that stand before her artistic integrity. But," and Noble suddenly pounded his fist on the desk in exasperation, "she was laughing at me all the time. She didn't mean any of that crap about artistic integrity."

"I know what you mean," Jake said. "Where did you go when you left her?"

Noble wet his lips and got to his feet. "I just went out and got drunk," he said. "I felt lousy, and one drink led to another. I heard the radio flash about May in the Croydon bar, so I called you, and then came over to the office. I—I realized that it would look bad if it came out that I'd been to May's. So I cooked up the story about being with Bebe for you, and hoped you'd cover up for me by saying we'd been together all night talking business."

Jake sighed. "I don't care very much, understand, but have you got any witnesses at these bars where you did your drinking? Do you have anybody who can back up your story?"

Noble made himself a drink and remained at the bar, stirring the liquor with one hand and rubbing

118

his forehead with the other. "You know how things like that are, Jake," he said, with a petulant frown. "You have a few drinks, and talk with somebody you don't want to talk to, and then you go out and drift somewhere else, and do the same thing. You're looking for somebody that wants to listen to you, but everybody wants to talk about himself, and then you look for a girl, and there aren't any, and you get drunker and sadder all the time and when it's all over it just adds up to nothing." He sighed despondently. "Who'd remember me? I'm just a fat man who wears loud ties and talks all the time."

"For God's sake, cut it out," Jake said, disgusted and amused at the same time. "Instead of all this corn, I'd suggest you backtrack your route of that night and look for someone who can support your story. The police will get to you eventually, and they'll want more than a dissertation on the bitter irony of solitary drinking."

"I'll do that," Noble said with a switch back to his normal vigor. "Now, you'd better check on how Niccolo is coming with that job for *Time*."

"Sure. First things first," Jake said, drily, and left Noble staring after him perplexedly.

Jake walked down to his office, careful to keep his eyes straight ahead when he passed Sheila's open door. He didn't feel up to an apology this early in the morning. The door between his office and Toni Ryerson's cubicle was open, and he saw that her neatly shod feet were in their customary position atop her desk. He walked into her office and said hello, and she immediately began badgering him with questions about Avery Meed's murder.

"I don't know a thing," he told her, with a shrug. "He was strangled with one of his own neckties and the murderer is still at large, as authors are found of saying."

Dean Niccolo came in through the other door to Toni's office, with a pipe in his mouth and grinning cheerfully. He sat down, stretched out his long legs, and nodded to Jake; and Toni, Jake noticed, colored and began to shift papers about on her desk with aimless efficiency.

Jake said, "How's the Riordan handout coming?"

"Pretty well," Niccolo said. "I'll have it ready by noon."

"I'll bet it's good," Toni said.

Jake wondered idly if she were in love with Niccolo. And glancing at him, tanned and muscular, with his dark features glowing with health, he decided she would be crazy if she weren't. There was a controlled and indolent power in Niccolo that was very provocative.

Niccolo smiled at her and said, "Why, thanks. Thanks a lot."

Toni beamed and Jake excused himself and returned to his office, closing the connecting door behind him. He found Toni's rapt reaction to Niccolo somewhat difficult to bear.

Lighting a cigarette, he walked restlessly to the window, observing with dour satisfaction the cold cheerless view of the boulevard and lake.

For a few minutes he tried to think about the Riordan account, but his thoughts slid away from that and settled on the circumstances of May's death.

The one 'fact' they had to work with, it seemed, was that Avery Meed had gone to see May at Riordan's request, and had come away with the diary. That was what Meed had told Riordan, at least. Meed might have lied to his boss, although there was no apparent reason for that, and Riordan might have lied to Lieutenant Martin, but, again, there was no reason for it. Taking everyone's word then, Meed had gone to May's home, had got the diary, and had come away with it.

Then had Meed murdered May?

There was one point that made that more than a possibility. Meed had intended to buy May off; and if he had been successful then the money or check should have been among May's effects. She would hardly have given him the diary on his promise to pay.

Therefore, since the police had found nothing of the sort, Meed must have taken the diary without paying for it—and he could hardly have done that while May was alive. Possibly, very possibly, it seemed, he might have made his offer, been refused and then been forced to kill her to get the diary.

The other possibility was that May had been dead when Meed arrived. If that were true, then May was murdered by someone with no interest in the diary, for it had been left for Meed to find.

All of this speculation led him no closer to the answers he wanted: Who killed May? Who killed Meed? Where was the diary?

There was still Mike Francesca unaccounted for, Jake knew. Mike, that amiable assassin, would have murdered May with a sigh of regret but without hesitation if it were necessary to his peace of mind and safety.

Jake's reflections were cut short by the ring of his phone. The receptionist told him Gregory Prior was waiting and wished to see him immediately.

"Send him in," Jake said, and settled back in his chair with a smile.

Prior appeared in the doorway of Jake's office a moment or so later, wearing an expression of grim and righteous anger on his face. He also wore a hard worsted, pepper-and-salt tweed suit, a white Oxford cloth shirt and a green wool knit tie.

"Well, this is pleasant," Jake said. "Sit down, won't you?"

"Thanks," Prior said, and sat down without relaxing

the stiffness of his body. "I won't take much of your time. I guess you've seen the morning papers."

"Why, yes," Jake said. "Why?"

"You know what I'm talking about. Did you see the *Tribune* editorial, for instance?"

Jake smiled innocently. "Now that you mention it, I remember it quite well. It mentioned you by name, I think. Said something about witch hunting, didn't it?"

"You can afford to be amused," Prior said bitterly. "Do you realize you've already, with that one editorial, convinced thousands of people that Riordan is merely being hounded by a snooping, bureaucratic committee?"

"Well, that was my fondest hope," Jake said mildly. "But, after all, I didn't write the editorial."

Prior's lips tightened. "I know you're responsible for the present attitude of the press on the Riordan investigation. Frankly, I can't understand people like you, Harrison. You're willing, even glad apparently, to defend a thieving war racketeer like Daniel Riordan. You'll do anything at all, I suppose, for money."

"That's a nice, simple way of putting it," Jake said equably.

Prior lit a cigarette with a quick, angry gesture; then, after inhaling deeply, he looked directly at Jake and said, "Ever have any trouble sleeping nights? Do you ever ask yourself what principles, if any, you

123

live by?"

"Oh, for God's sake," Jake said. "I don't lure small children into alleys, and I don't speak snidely of Free Enterprise, and I sleep wonderfully. What that has to do with the subject, however, escapes me. Getting to the point, I suggested we work harmoniously on this account, but you ignored that and, at the first opportunity, sounded off to the papers in a manner that made Riordan look like a culprit. So I hit back. You seem to want to know why I did; well, now you know."

Prior shook his head with a gesture of controlled desperation. "You talk as if this were a boxing match. Don't you understand that my job is to track down a man who has cheated and defrauded his country in time of war, has cost the lives of American soldiers to fatten his own bank accounts? You're distorting and impeding that work because you're paid to do so, and I say it's scandalous."

"Oh, relax a minute," Jake said. "You're annoyed because you've been held up as a symbol of fascistic bureaucracy. Well, that's a bit thick, of course. But even if I weren't paid to think so at the moment, I'd have a low opinion of your committee and particularly its eminent chairman, Senator Hampstead. He's always struck me as a tyrannical, prudish old bastard. But the important thing right now is that Riordan has not been charged with any crimes, and until he is, and until that charge is proved by due process of law, then it's my job and my duty to defend him from the mudslinging innuendoes, and damnation-by-association tactics of you Washington ferrets."

"Do you actually believe that?" Prior asked.

Jake let out his breath slowly. For a second he wished he could feel convinced he was doing a job because it was the right thing to do; he wished he was standing on the side of the angels. But of course he wasn't.

"No, I don't believe that," he said shortly. "I'm a press agent. And public relations is a process which takes money from a client, and puts it in the pocket of a press agent. But as long as you have no case against Riordan, then my position is proportionately stronger. Until you get some evidence, I'll just knock you silly in the papers every day."

"Okay, then, listen to this," Prior said, putting out his cigarette with a curiously deliberate gesture. "I came to Chicago as Senator Hampstead's represent-ative, to investigate a contract Riordan made with the Army to produce one-hundred-and-fifty-five-millimeter gun barrels. Do you know how we got on his trail? No, you probably don't know, or care. We received reports from theater commanders in the ETO, reports which had come to them through company, regiment, and division commanders, about barrels which cracked and split during combat firing.

It took time to coordinate these reports, to determine what firm had supplied most of the defective barrels, and to get ordnance reports on the quality of the metal recovered from those burst guns. That was a long painstaking job and when it was completed we saw that Dan Riordan's company had made most of those barrels.

"Now we're moving in on him. Already our first check into his books tells us that he arbitrarily ignored his contracts with the army. He used a cheaper grade of steel, a steel that cracked under the heat and pressure of firing."

Jake fingered his letter opener and shrugged slightly. "You probably have more information than I do, Prior. But Riordan told me that much himself. He said it was a question of using cheaper steel or of making no barrels at all. He preferred using the cheaper steel."

"Sure, he would," Prior said, harshly. "Because he charged the government for the price of the high-quality steel. Riordan owns, among other things, a casting company and a steel mill. He bought cheap steel from his mill, the Sterling Steel Corporation, and made a profit on the sale, and then he put that cheap steel into the barrels made by the Riordan Casting Company. When he sold those barrels—supposedly made of high-grade steel—he collected a double profit, the first on the sale from his mill to his steel company, and secondly by unloading that inferior material at a price paid for the very best steel."

"You've worked pretty fast," Jake said, pointlessly; he didn't know what else to say.

"We're still working, too," Prior said, grimly. "We also know that Riordan bribed a government plant inspector, a man named Nickerson, to okay the faulty barrels. When we catch up with Nickerson we'll have a case that Riordan will never wriggle out of. Possibly you can understand my irritation now. Maybe I sounded like a stuffed shirt coming in here to complain about your doing your job, but we know what kind of a client you've got—and it hurts to be made a fool of when you're in the right."

"Of course," Jake said, absently. He was thinking that the agency would have to change its pitch on Riordan now. Jake hadn't thought much about Riordan's guilt or innocence, but he had felt that if Riordan were guilty he would have covered things so he wouldn't be caught. Obviously, he was not only a crook, but a stupid one.

"Why don't you simply lock him up, if you've got him cold?" Jake asked.

"First of all, that's not our job. My report goes to the Senator who, in spite of your feeling, is an able and conscientious man, and he decides whether or not his committee will investigate the matter thoroughly. When that investigation is over, the Attorney

General will move in to prosecute. And our case right now is not fully completed. We won't get through his books for several more weeks."

Prior stood up abruptly and smiled at Jake, "You probably think I'm a very naive person to come here like this and raise hell with you for making me look like a fool in the papers. Perhaps I did sound off to the reporters without thinking. Maybe we can have lunch some day, if you're not tied up, and stop fighting each other."

"Of course," Jake said. He found himself rather admiring Prior's frankness, although he was normally dismayed by honest people, because they were an erratic element in the well-ordered and hypocritical world of business.

They walked down the corridor to the reception room together, and Jake found his thoughts turning to May again, as they seemed to inexorably now. He said, "Here's something I'd like to talk to you about. May Laval was a friend of mine, and I talked with her the night before she was killed. I knew about the diary she'd kept and what she intended doing with it, of course, and I asked her to lay off Riordan. She said she was going ahead with the book, not to spite Riordan, particularly, but because it was a thing she had to do. Now, what changed her mind? She called you later that night, didn't she?"

"Well, she called my assistant, Coombs. About one

in the morning, I think. She said she had some information that we might find useful. Coombs told me and I called her and made a date for the following morning. The next morning we learned she'd been killed. I understand from the papers that now a man named Avery Meed has been killed, and that he had the diary."

"That's right," Jake said. "But the diary is still missing."

"Well, perhaps it will turn up. I'd like to see it, you know. You say you knew this May Laval. What sort of a person was she?"

Jake shrugged. "That's a difficult question," he said.

They entered the reception room and Prior stopped with his hand on the doorknob. "Judging from the papers she was simply a rather glorified prostitute."

"That's not quite accurate," Jake said.

"Well, I didn't mean to sound stuffy," Prior said hastily. "But the picture one gets second hand is hardly that of a convent-bred little miss. The papers are playing that up pretty strong, of course." He smiled at Jake as he said this, but his eyes were cool. "The papers have a habit of distorting things, I know," he said.

"Let's not start that again," Jake said. "Getting back to May: She was a generous friend, and could be loyal, warm-hearted and amusing. Her vice was that she needed attention, and worked a bit too hard getting it."

"Yes, I saw her home, you know," Prior said. "She apparently used everything from her red pajamas to her furniture with the thought of hitting you squarely in the eye. Her book would undoubtedly have been wonderful reading. But tell me this; the papers said Meed took the diary from her home. Does that mean he killed her?"

"It's a thought," Jake said. "It's undoubtedly occurred to the police."

"Yes, it's an obvious idea," Prior said.

They were both silent a moment, and then Prior smiled at Jake, and said, "We're in the Postal Building if you should want me. . . ."

The receptionist waved to Jake as he turned from the door and started back to his office.

"I have a call for you. You can take it here, if you like."

"Thanks," Jake said.

To his considerable surprise it was Denise Riordan. They talked of unimportant things for a while, and then she said, "I would like to talk with you this afternoon. Do you have any free time?"

"Why, of course. How about two thirty, here at the office?"

"Couldn't we have a drink somewhere? Offices are too functional to suit me."

Jake raised an eyebrow at the phone. "All right." He thought a moment, remembered an invitation to a cocktail party that had been in the morning mail. "How about the lobby of the Palmer House at two thirty?"

"That's fine."

Jake put the phone down and wondered what the devil Denise Riordan wanted to see him about. He didn't like the idea of rendezvousing with clients' wives. It was unpolitic.

Walking back to his office he decided that the time had come to make amends with Sheila, so he stopped at her office. She was working at her desk, looking cool and lovely in a gray suit with a red flower pinned to the left lapel.

"I'm sorry about last night," he said. "I was pretty much of a damn fool, I suppose."

"Don't be sophomoric, Jake," Sheila looked up and smiled briefly. "I was wrong last night, too. It's none of my business what you think and believe."

"And never the twain shall meet, eh?" Jake said.

"I think you've used me as an ersatz conscience long enough," Sheila said, looking down at her desk. "Maybe you've felt that if one of us disapproved of some of the things you've done with the agency, that was enough. I'm through being an indulgent mother to you."

"Let's talk it over when I get rid of this hangover,"

131

Jake said moodily. "This is like having a cop tell you he doesn't care what you do."

"I'm no cop," Sheila said. "You can break all the windows in the block from now on, and I'll have no objections."

"Whee!" Jake said in a listless voice.

He walked back slowly to his office.

CHAPTER NINE

It was eleven thirty. Jake sat at his desk, staring at the leather-bound clock for several minutes without moving. He knew he should be working. The agency would need something spectacular in the way of a campaign if Riordan were guilty. And Prior quite obviously knew Riordan was guilty and had the proof in names and dates to back up his charge.

But he didn't feel like working. He thought about May again and finally decided to take a trip out to Mike Francesca's farm.

Barrington was a horsy suburb of Chicago that had become popular for people who wanted something slightly more rugged in appearance than country club or station wagon living. In Barrington there were farms of twenty or twenty-five acres, usually run by tenant farmers who did all the work; and comfortable homes representing all varieties of architectural importation, from Maine salt boxes to Mexican haciendas. Tennis courts and swimming pools clustered around these houses with a cheerful, unmortgaged look.

Jake told his cab driver to wait and walked down the gravel path that led to Francesca's place, a sprawling ranch house of impressive dimensions.

A stockily built man wearing a leather windbreaker stepped around the side of the house and sauntered down to meet him.

"Who'd you want, pal?" he said amiably.

"I'd like to see Mike. I'm a friend, Jake Harrison." He recognized the man and smiled. "You're Yeabo Jones, aren't you?"

"Yeah, how'd you know?" the man said.

"I covered your trial in thirty-eight. You got six years for armed robbery and aggravated assault and battery."

"Oh, yeah," Yeabo Jones said. "You was a reporter, eh?"

"That's right."

"Well, come on up to the house and I'll see what the boss says."

Yeabo told him to wait at the door while he went inside. Jake lit a cigarette and looked up at the bare elms and cold steel sky.

Yeabo opened the door behind him and said, "Come on in."

Mike Francesca was seated in a large chair before a log fire, wearing soft gray flannel slacks and a gab-

134

ardine sport shirt with hand-stitched lapels and cuffs. He got to his feet when Jake entered, and came to meet him, a wide smile wreathing his face into a network of wrinkles. There was another person, a show-girl style of blonde, lying before the fireplace with a Martini at her elbow. She sat up tailor-fashion and regarded Jake solemnly.

"Jake, you old son-of-a-gun," Mike said, wringing his hand. "Nice of you to blow in like this. You know Cheryl, huh?"

"Why, no. But it's a pleasure."

"It's Cheryl Dane," the girl said. "He thinks I'm a horse or something with just a first name."

"Well," Mike said, smiling at her, "what do you need with two names? One's good enough for any-body." He took Jake's elbow and pushed him toward a chair. "Now sit down and we'll have a drink. Yeabo!" He sang out the last word loudly and the blonde winced.

Yeabo brought wine for Mike and Jake had a Martini. When he disappeared Mike settled back in his chair with a comfortable sigh. "This is good, eh?" he said.

"Fine," Jake said, and sipped his drink.

"Anything in particular on your mind?" Mike asked.

"Yes, there is," Jake said slowly. "I'm wondering if you know anything about who killed May Laval. I know you were worried about her book, and—"

"And you think I had her killed, eh?" Mike said. "That's right, eh?"

The blonde rolled over on her back and crossed her long and well-shaped legs. "You know, Mike," she said. "I'd—"

"Shut up," he said, without glancing at her, and she shrugged and became silent.

"You think maybe I had May killed, eh?" Mike said.

"No, I don't think that at all," Jake said. "If you'd killed her you'd have gotten the diary, I think."

Mike tapped his forehead significantly. "See, you got a good head."

"I suppose you're looking for the diary now?"

"Oh, yes, my boys are looking for it. I think they'll get it, too."

"Do you have any guess as to who killed May?"

"You know that is very funny," Mike said, frowning and touching his lower lip with a forefinger. "Who should kill her, eh? I've thought about that a lot, all the time in fact since she was killed. And I don't know. You know May and I used to play poker in the old days. Me, May, Ed Hogan, the alderman, and a bartender at the old Troy Club. May, she was a real son-of-a-gun." Mike shook his head gently. "Mother of Heaven, what games! May could shove a thousand dollars into the pot and grin at you, when she had nothing, not even a pair. Ah, what days we had then, eh?"

"Yah, yah," the blonde said. "I never met one of you guys from Prohibition days who didn't act like fat men at a college reunion."

"She's real cute, eh?" Mike said.

"Well, what's this poker game got to do with May's death?" Jake said.

"Oh, nothing," Mike said, with a tired wave of his hand. "But nobody minded losing to May. Oh, the money it was too bad to lose, but nobody got real mad. She was liked, eh? And that's why I wonder about who could kill her."

Jake shrugged. "Wouldn't you have killed her, Mike?"

Mike took his arm and they walked to the door together. "I'll tell you a secret," he said.

"What's that?"

"I would have very quick," Mike said.

"That's what I thought."

"Ha!" Mike said, and tapped his forehead again. "You got the head, Jake."

"Thanks. Goodbye, Mike."

"Goodbye."

Jake walked down the drive, drawing his overcoat tight around him against the cold hard wind that was blowing. The cab driver turned into the driveway and Jake climbed in and lit a cigarette while the driver backed up to turn around.

They were ready to pull out when a shout from

the house made the driver stop. Jake looked out and saw Yeabo running toward them with a gallon jug of pale brown liquid in each hand.

Jake opened his door and said, "What the hell is that?" as Yeabo came up beside the car.

"Cider," Yeabo panted. "We make it right here. The boss wants you to have it."

"Tell him it's just what I wanted," Jake said.

Driving back to the city, the driver glanced over his shoulder and said, "That's a real friendly gesture, I'd say. I mean it's kind of old-fashioned to give guests something like that to take with them."

"My friend is of the old school," Jake said. "But I'm not. Would you like it—the cider, I mean?"

The cab driver said that would be fine, and Jake said okay, and told him to drive to the Palmer House.

He sat back wondering what was on Denise Riordan's mind.

Jake went up the steps leading to the lobby of the Palmer House and after a quick glance around saw her sitting in a chair beside a tall palm and idly turning the pages of a fashion magazine. She was wearing a black faille dress with broad amber earrings and choker, and her eyes were very bright against her tanned skin.

"Why, hello," she said, standing. "You're punctual."

"Men my age have to cultivate minor virtues to

compensate for our lack of major vices," Jake said, and realized that he sounded roguish.

He suggested a drink and they went upstairs to a private room on the mezzanine where some thirty or forty young men and women were standing about and drinking liquor provided by radio station WXL.

Jake got two drinks from the bar and led Denise to a green satin sofa. She sat down rather cautiously and he realized that she had been drinking. Her movements were somewhat too deliberate.

WXL's press agent, an energetic and beaming young man named Miller stopped by and wrung Jake's hand and asked if everything were all right. He nodded to Denise and then with a quick smile and a glance at her long slender legs, excused himself and joined another group.

"Is he the host?" Denise asked.

"I suppose you could call him that." He held a match to her cigarette and said, "Now what burning motive prompted you to call me?"

Denise smiled. "You'll think I'm foolish. But I liked you. And my life gets very dull at times. So I thought I'd get to know you better. It's as simple as that."

"That's very flattering. But I can't believe your life is dull."

Denise sipped her drink and patted his arm. The gesture was oddly intimate, and Jake had the ridiculous feeling that he was going to start edging away from her any minute.

"Danny is busy most of the time, you know," she said, smiling. "He's an old-fashioned husband. He thinks a woman is part of the equipment in a well-run home."

"Let me fix your drink," Jake interrupted, just to be saying something uncompromising, and left her long enough to get two fresh drinks.

She was glancing at the other people at the party with interest when he returned, and had apparently forgotten her husband and Jake as conversational gambits.

She said, "Where in the name of God do all these brilliant young bastards come from and what are they doing here?"

"Well, this is a business cocktail party and these young people work for advertising agencies. The station hopes to obligate them to the extent of a few highballs, so that when their agencies buy time they will remember WXL fondly."

"Does it work out that way?"

"Sometimes, I suppose. But mostly not." He glanced up at the crowd. "I don't see anyone here who could make a decision on anything more important than taking an extra comma from a piece of copy."

"They sound very smart," Denise said with a dubious nod of her head.

They did indeed, Jake reflected. The air was thick

with the inside of "inside" stories, and the scraps of conversation that fell around him sparkled with epigrammatic criticisms of all art forms, of all entertainment, of damn near everything. Two young men directly in front of them were arguing heatedly about an article from the *Partisan Review*, a piece, Jake gathered, which advanced the theory that all homes flourished for the purpose of gratifying the father's and mother's need for an incestuous relationship within a socially approved framework; behind them a scoop of Drew Pearson's was belittled as having told only half the story, and the unpublished half was being recounted scornfully by a man who wrote jingles for Curvex Foundation Garments; a group of three young girls and two middle-aged men were giggling over the things one of the men was saying about prominent writers; he had said that Truman Capote was a nasty little boy scribbling four-syllable words on the sidewalk, and that Hemingway's self-conscious virility stemmed from his having been drummed from the Boy Scouts as a youth, and that William Saroyan was really Norman Corwin with a coating of glucose; and in the corner a young man with lank dark hair was telling a captivated girl that the war had shot his integration right to hell. "I crystallized between satyrism and impotence," he added angrily.

"Can I have a drink?" Denise said. "These people

are terrific. I feel like the real bourgeois."

"It's just talk," Jake said. "Really, it's a trick."

He brought her a drink which she finished quickly. They talked casually for a few moments, and then she said, "Aren't you bored with me?"

"Why, no. Not at all."

"Spoken like a gentleman." She was quite tight, Jake saw. Her bright blue eyes focused on his intently. "You're thinking I'm just the drunk and aging wife of a client, aren't you? Somebody you'd damn well better be nice to."

"No, I wasn't thinking anything of the sort," Jake said.

"Well, what are you thinking? You're not thinking of me by any remote chance, are you?"

"Yes, I was thinking of you," Jake said, and smiled. He wanted now to get her home. "I was thinking a drive might be pleasant."

"God, that's a feverish thought," Denise laughed. "You've got to be more controlled, Mr. Harrison. Keep that wild Latin temperament of yours in check."

"I'm not called the North American continent for nothing," Jake said, hoping the gag, old and undistinguished though it was, might get her in a better humor.

"Oh, yah, yah, yah," Denise said. "You think I'm a bore. Just a dumb babe on the make. Well, I know something that might surprise you. Danny thinks

142

you're doing a lousy job for him."

"Well, he's right," Jake said. "But it's a tough account."

"Also I know something about your great and glorious May Laval." She bowed her head in mock solemnity. "Everyone has to do that when they mention her name, you know. She was so damn witty and clever and wonderful and now she's so damn dead. Isn't that a laugh?"

"I suppose it has an element of humor in it," Jake said.

"Oh, don't bother making me feel ashamed. You're wasting your time."

"But what do you know about her?" Jake said.

"I know that Danny Boy sent Avery Meed to her apartment to get her diary. Now, isn't that delightful news?"

Jake felt let down. That much Riordan had already admitted. But he was curious as to how Denise knew as much as she did, and hopeful that she might know more. So he said, "You're doing fine, but you'll have to do better than that to shock me."

Denise said, "I don't know anything else." She sipped the last of her drink. "You see, Danny Boy does a lot of business from home by phone, so I listen in on the extension by my bed. That's the only way I can find out anything, and it's better than listening to a radio."

"I see. And you heard Danny Boy tell Meed to go to May's apartment and get the diary?"

"That's right. And he was really mad. He told Meed to get that diary or else."

"Or else what?"

Denise said, "Well, I don't know. Everybody says do something-or-other 'or else.' Nobody ever asks 'or else what?' It's a good question."

"Well, go on. Then Danny Boy left for Gary?"

"No, he didn't leave until the next call. You see," she went on, talking very deliberately now, as if she were explaining long division to a six-year-old. "You see, Avery Meed called Danny Boy back, and said he had the diary. And he said he had something else to talk to Danny Boy about. I was kind of sleepy then, and didn't hear much else. But that's the way it was," she concluded firmly.

Jake lit another cigarette and tried to keep his voice casual. "Where was Danny Boy between those two calls?"

"He was in the living-room. You see, I was in bed."

"You didn't see him between those two calls? I mean he didn't come into your bedroom?"

"Sure, just as he was leaving for Gary." She frowned. "That was *after* the second call, though. He said he was going out to Gary, and he told me—"

She stopped suddenly and a look of dismay flickered across her face. For a moment she stared at Jake, and then she laughed nervously.

"Did he tell you to remember that he'd left for Gary earlier—much earlier—in the evening?" Jake said gently.

Denise looked at him and then shook her head. "I didn't realize how much I'd drunk. I'm having pipe dreams. Would you take me home?"

"Wouldn't you rather talk, or perhaps go some place where it's quiet? I find you very fascinating all of a sudden."

"No, I'd rather go home. You're not being very bright, you know."

"You're the one who talked out of school," Jake said.

"I might talk a little more to Danny," she said.

"I doubt if that would help. Come on, let's go."

They went down to the lobby where Denise became a very unsteady package to handle; and Jake wondered if she were really that drunk, or just pretending to avoid talking with him.

If she had told him the truth then Riordan's alibi was shot; he had been in town at the time of May's death. Jake realized then that they had only Riordan's word for Avery Meed's part in the story. Riordan might have killed May, and then invented a story that made Meed look guilty. After that he could kill Meed and the police would have their culprit and be satisfied. The heat would be off and Riordan would be free and clear.

It was all so possible that Jake felt slightly cold thinking about it.

When they finally reached the Riordan suite at the Blackstone, he felt as if he had been through a stiff, cross-country race. He fished the key from Denise's purse and let them in. There seemed to be no one at home, for which Jake silently thanked God.

Denise sagged against him as he helped her inside and got the door shut. But she revived when she realized that she was home.

"Drink, Jake?" she said cheerfully.

Disengaging herself from him with a conspiratorial smile, she made for the liquor cabinet, with a slight list to port; but she changed her mind on the way and pirouetted with surprising grace toward the long couch that ran under the windows. Sinking onto it with one foot trailing on the floor, she said, "There is no place like home, after all," in a wondering voice, and closed her eyes.

Jake was lighting a cigarette when he heard a key in the door. He shrugged philosophically and turned as Dan Riordan let himself in, looking preoccupied.

"Well, what's this?" he said. "What's wrong with her?" he said, glancing at Jake.

"We had a drink this afternoon, and I think Denise had one too many. She's okay. Just sleepy."

"I see," Riordan said.

He walked to her side and shook her shoulder. She

opened her eyes and said plaintively, "Okay, Muscles, knock it off."

"You'd better go to your room," he said.

She struggled to a sitting position, looking contrite. "Don't be that way, Danny Boy. I—I just picked up a little load, that's all."

Riordan said, in a softer tone, "All right, but you'll be more comfortable in your room."

Denise stood up and clung to him until she became accustomed to the perpendicular position. "I was just having a little fun, Danny." Placing her arm around his neck she kissed him on the mouth.

Riordan put his hand on her waist and they stood together for a moment. When he released her, there was a smile on his face.

"You're so nice to me, Danny," she said sleepily. "Let's go off somewhere for a while and be together. Let's go to the lodge again and swim in the moonlight and make love before the big fire. Please, Danny."

"You want to go to the lodge again, eh?"

"Oh, yes, Danny Boy," she said and put her head on his shoulder.

Riordan put an arm about her waist and led her through the arched doorway of the living room. He returned in a few moments.

"Do you want a drink?" he said to Jake.

"No, thanks. But I'd like to talk to you."

"Okay, go ahead," Riordan said.

"I've just had a talk with Prior, the Government investigator."

"Oh," Riordan said. "I thought you might be going to explain how you and my wife happened to be spending the afternoon together, and how she got drunk."

Jake said, "We spent the afternoon together at a cocktail party, because she phoned and asked me if I'd like to have a drink. She got drunk by the not too difficult expedient of lifting a fresh drink to her mouth fifteen or twenty times. You know damn well, Riordan, that people get themselves drunk. Let's get back to Prior."

Riordan looked at Jake appraisingly for a moment. "You're smart. If you'd had any mealy-mouthed apologies about this afternoon I'd have tossed you out on your ear. But I know Denise, and I know this afternoon wasn't your fault."

"That's two of us convinced of my purity," Jake said drily. "Now to get back to Prior; he seems to think he's got you cold."

Riordan shrugged impatiently.

"I know. He's found an ink blot somewhere in my books and he's going to send me to jail. There's no one more officious than a four-thousand-dollar-a-year Government clerk, when he thinks he can annoy a man with money."

"This seems to be more than an ink spot," Jake

said. "Here's Prior's story: Your contract for 155 mm. gun barrels specified a certain grade of steel. He thinks you used a cheaper grade, which you bought from your own mill, but charged the government for the price of the specified steel. Also, he told me that you bribed a plant inspector, by the name of Nickerson, to okay the defective barrels."

"When did he tell you this?"

"About eleven thirty this morning."

Riordan laughed humorlessly. "They're working like beavers, aren't they? Are they looking for this fellow Nickerson?"

"Yes."

"Fine," Riordan said. "Nickerson died a couple of years ago. They'll get a lot from him, won't they?"

"They seem to have all they need without him."

Riordan looked at him shrewdly. "Let's understand each other, Harrison. You're on my side because you're getting paid. I may be a crook for all you know, but that doesn't make my money less valuable. But you may have scruples. Do you stay on the team or get off?"

"That's a pointless question," Jake said, wearily. "I'm your press counsel, remember? I can't talk effectively to editors unless you give me straight information. You haven't done that so far. First you sent Avery Meed to May's to get the diary after telling me you'd let me handle the matter. Now Prior tells me a story about your operations that differs from yours on several important points. I can't do you any good unless you keep me briefed on what's happening, and tell me a straight story about your dealings with the Government."

"That makes sense," Riordan said. "You want to know how much of Prior's story is true, I suppose. Actually, it makes no difference to you one way or the other, does it? Your loyalty is for sale and I'm buying it. I intend that you work just as hard for me if I'm a crook as you would if I were honest. That satisfactory to you?"

"Yes, that's quite satisfactory," Jake said after a pause.

"Fine. I like realistic people, Harrison. The world is glutted with fools who refuse to accept the simple, blunt facts of life. The world makes heroes of successful people. But it doesn't put the credit where it belongs. Successful people get praised for going to school under polar conditions, or endowing a transept in a church, or for uttering some bromidic nonsense about their mothers. The truth is they should be praised for their rapacity, their single-minded absorption with making money, for those are the things that send you up the ladder, and they always have, in every country, in every age." Riordan put a cigar in his mouth, lighted it, and laughed. "Don't bother reading history. Just look around at the names in America that you see on libraries, churches and boulevards. And remember how their money was made. You should have spent some time in Washington during the war. By God, you could write a book about it. If I wrote it I'd call it 'The Pig Trough.' That's what it was. Just a big pig trough with everyone grunting around and digging his snout into the garbage as far as he could.

"But to get back to Prior; he's bluffing. He's got no case against me and he's getting desperate."

Jake thought of asking Riordan bluntly about his whereabouts the night of May's murder. But as he had lied to the police there was small likelihood he'd change his story now for Jake. He walked to the door and Riordan came with him and shook hands with him strongly.

"Don't be a worrier, Jake," Riordan said. "I don't like worried people around me. They exude defeat. Nobody can touch me, remember that."

"Okay," Jake said. "I'll remember that."

He walked down to the elevators thinking over what Riordan had said, and wondering why he hadn't advanced any argument against Riordan's point of view. Once in his life he would have. But now he wasn't in any position to, he perceived. Riordan was a crook and a thief; but he was running his errands. You couldn't impose a moral judgment on anyone whose money was jingling in your pocket.

CHAPTER TEN

He stopped for a Scotch and soda at the Blackstone bar and smoked a cigarette while he drank it. He hadn't enjoyed the session with Riordan. It was not pleasant to be told bluntly that your loyalty was for sale. But that's what it amounted to, so there was no point in being annoyed. It was merely the process of supply and demand at work.

When he went outside to get a cab another idea occurred to him. He could regain Prior's good will by telling what he'd learned of Nickerson; namely, that the man was dead. That would save Prior the time of making an investigation, and it couldn't possibly hurt Riordan.

Waiting on the curb in the cold gray weather it occurred to him that he didn't particularly want to ingratiate himself with Prior. He considered Prior a dedicated young ass. Yet it was necessary for him to make a placating overture, because Riordan might need even the tiniest speck of good will from Prior when things got grim.

It was, all things considered, an undistinguished sort of business.

Prior's unit was installed in a suite of offices on the eighteenth floor of the Postal Building. A busy young man in the reception room told Jake that Prior was in conference and couldn't be disturbed. Jake said he'd wait a moment and took a seat.

There was a door directly before him that led to a private office, and the transom above the door was open. Through this aperture a high-pitched irascible voice suddenly sounded:

"Excuses, gentlemen, are the base coin with which incompetents hope to buy the respect of conscientious men."

The young man at the desk glanced at Jake and then up at the open transom before returning to his work with noticeably renewed energy.

The voice continued stridently: "The papers in this city have joined in excoriating your work, and I refuse to believe that this unanimity of opinion is traceable to anything but some egregious mistake in your procedure."

"Senator Hampstead has arrived, I hear," Jake said, recognizing the voice.

"That's right," the young man said, and smiled politely. "The tempo picks up a little when he's around."

"I can imagine."

Jake had met Elias Hampstead, senior Senator from a midwestern state, several times in Washington and Chicago. He had considered him a windbag, a charlatan, and a bore; but the Senator had a staunch and zealous national following.

Senator Hampstead had a reputation among his followers for selfless honesty, unflinching rectitude, and deathless integrity; and for being, by actual count, at least a one hundred and fifteen per cent dyed-in-the-wool American.

He had been elected in the twenties on a fusion ticket which had as its platform the reëstablishment of the pioneer principles of godliness and decency. No one took the campaign seriously except Elias Hampstead, who at the time was in his early forties and had lost his farm in the depression following the first World War. He had been selling religious pamphlets to care for his wife and son, when the political movement swept him up and gave him a reason for taking up space on earth.

He was elected to the Senate and immediately sponsored bills which respectively advocated the abolishment of horse racing, dog racing, prize fighting, professional baseball, and drinking. He became the butt of a thousand gags and cartoons. He was railed at as the personification of prudery, the epitome of provincial insularity. But there was something about his stubbornness, his boorishness, his refusal to stop braying forth his pious platitudes for even a moment, that perversely caused some people to admire him; and among certain cheerless sects he came to be looked upon as a sort of down-to-earth, home-spun Messiah.

Near the close of the war the Hampstead Committee was formed to investigate war profits and the breath of fear blew across the back of anyone it turned its attention to, because this committee was as harsh in its judgments as the laws of the Old Testament. The committee took its character from Senator Hampstead. He was incorruptible. His past was without a flaw or stain. He had lived for thirty years with a gray, retiring woman who had died shortly after their only son was killed in the war. He had no unexplained bank accounts. He was the militant foe of lewdness, of corruption, of wrong doing, of anything, in short, that differed from his concept of decency, modesty and godliness.

Such was the man, Jake thought with a humorless smile, who would weigh the evidence against Dan Riordan. It would be difficult to imagine two men more opposed in their tastes, convictions and motivations.

The door of the private office opened and Senator Hampstead emerged, trailed by Gregory Prior and Gil Coombs.

The Senator was a commonplace-looking man, with

straight, graying hair, appraising eyes, and features somewhat too small and bunched together to be handsome, but which were not unrefined. He was of middle height and his body was spare and well cared for. He wore a gray suit and carried a walking stick.

Jake said, "Hello, Senator. We've met before. My name is Harrison."

"Oh, yes," Senator Hampstead said. His normal voice was high, affected and irritating. "You're handling the public relations of that poltroon, Riordan, aren't you?"

"That's right," Jake said, easily.

"You've made our job difficult with your tactics. There should be a law that would permit us to lock up men like you."

"Why don't you introduce one?" Jake asked. He felt pleasantly angry. "It would hardly be noticed with the rest of your crackpot legislation."

"Good day," Senator Hampstead said slowly. And Jake knew he had hurt the man, and that he would never be forgiven. "Come along, Prior," the Senator said.

"All right," Prior said. He gave Jake a quick glance and shrugged helplessly as he followed the Senator from the office.

Coombs grinned at Jake. "The Senator is in a rare mood today. Come in, won't you? No need for us to bark at each other, at any rate?"

Inside the private office Jake saw neat stacks of ledgers and account books on two conference tables. "The Riordan records," Coombs said, running a hand through his thin hair. "Helluva job going through them. And it's mine, all mine," he added with a smile.

"No help?"

"Oh, yes. I'm just looking for sympathy. I have three accountants helping me, and Greg—Mr. Prior—takes care of the legal angles and runs the main show. Did you wish to see him?"

"Yes, but I can leave the message with you. He was looking for a man named Nickerson, who worked in a Riordan plant during the war as a Government inspector."

"Oh, yes?"

"Well, Nickerson is dead. I thought that would save you some time to know that. That information comes from Riordan, so it's probably accurate."

Coombs smiled. "Riordan must be a fascinating man." He glanced at the books on the tables. "Very bold, very venturesome, very adroit. That's the impression I'm getting. But I'd better make a note of that fellow's name. What was it?" He made a record of it on his memorandum pad.

They talked desultorily for a few moments then and Coombs mentioned that he was enjoying Chicago.

"It's an amazing city," he said. "I've been completely fascinated by some obscure bars on the South

Side. The music is genuine, honest-to-God jazz, and the people are just fabulous. We've also tried your West Side steak houses, and some of the West Madison Street bistros, but for color only, of course."

"You've got around," Jake said.

"Yes, Greg is a good guide," Coombs smiled.

Jake gave him the names and addresses of a few little-known places that were favorites of his, and Coombs made a note of them with an enthusiasm that Jake found rather charming.

"We've been to one of these, I think," Coombs said, "but we'll try the others if we can find the time. With Senator Hampstead on hand that will be difficult."

"I can imagine," Jake said.

They talked desultorily for a moment after that and finally Jake said goodbye to Coombs and went out to the elevators. He glanced at his watch and realized that the working day was about over.

It was five o'clock when he reached the office, and the receptionist told him that Mr. Noble had gone for the day, and also that a package had come for him in the afternoon which the office boy had delivered to his desk.

Jake thanked her and went to his office. He felt tired and depressed, and was glad that he'd missed Noble. There was something wrong with him, he knew.

The package was lying on his desk, a flat object

about twelve inches by twelve and two inches thick, wrapped in brown paper and tied clumsily but firmly with strong twine. Jake sat down, untied the knots and tore off the wrapping paper.

The package contained a large leather-bound book. Jake stared at it for a moment without recognition; and then he realized where he had seen it before and a cold tremor went down his back.

This was May's diary.

Jake sat for a moment holding the diary in his hands, and the only thought in his mind was that two people had died because of what it contained.

From the adjoining office he heard Toni Ryerson humming tunelessly, and he saw that her silken ankles were in their customary position atop her desk. He put the diary down and walked to the doorway that connected his office with Toni's.

"Mind if I close this door?" he said. "The draft through here is reaching the typhoon class."

"I'll try to live," Toni said.

Jake smiled and closed the door. Returning to his desk he picked up the diary and opened it to page one, which was dated the first of January, 1943.

Flipping to the back of the book he saw that it ended on December 31st, 1948. It was a six-year diary, with each page containing space for three days.

He frowned, trying to guess why the diary had been sent to him, of all people. Assuming for a start that Avery Meed had killed May to get the diary, whoever had sent it to him must be the person who had murdered Meed. But why in God's name should anyone kill Meed to get the diary, and then mail it to someone else?

Jake opened the diary to the last half of 1944, which was the time that Riordan had known May, and he immediately saw that someone had been at work with scissors. There were pages cut from the diary in every month from June through December of 1944. And it didn't take him long to see that there was no mention at all of Riordan in May's diary.

Jake looked at the obvious conclusion for a moment; someone had removed all reference to Riordan from the diary. That could have been Avery Meed. Or it could have been done by the person who murdered him.

For a few minutes he turned this idea over in his head, and then he picked up his phone and called Sheila's office. When she answered, he asked her if she would step down to his office for a moment. She hesitated, almost imperceptibly, before saying yes.

She appeared half a minute later, wearing a coat, and carrying her bag and gloves. "I was just leaving when you called," she said.

Jake closed the door behind her and picked up May's diary from his desk. "I wanted you to see this."

Sheila glanced at the book and then opened it

and began reading. For a few seconds her face was expressionless; but suddenly she caught her breath sharply.

"Where did you get this?" she asked.

"It came in the mail."

"Who sent it?"

"I have no idea."

She sat down carefully in the chair behind his desk. "What does it mean, Jake?"

"I'm not sure," he said. "However, it opens up some interesting ideas. Riordan, you know, sent Avery Meed to get the diary from May. Then someone murdered Meed later that morning and took off with the diary. Whoever sent this to me is probably the person who murdered Meed."

"Have you looked through it yet?"

"That's another thing." He leaned over her shoulder and opened the diary to the last half of 1944. "You'll notice that someone is collecting Riordaniana. There's no mention of him in the diary now."

She said, "Then whoever murdered Meed probably has the dirt on Riordan now."

"That's possible."

"What are you going to do with it?"

Jake grinned ironically. "What do you think I'm going to do?" he said. "I'm going to take a look at how our betters behaved themselves during the war."

He opened the diary to page one.

May's account of her wartime relationships with gangsters, industrialists, artists, movie stars, generals and prostitutes was a fascinating chronicle, Jake realized after reading only a few pages. She recounted verbatim conversations and her memory for names, dates and places had been amazing. There was the saga of a three-star general whose name had become a household symbol for idealism and unflinching honesty during the war, but who, according to May's record of his comments while drinking, was actually little more than an office boy for one of the nation's major industries. And her account of the relationship between a politician of national stature and a foreign ambassador could have footnoted a chapter in Kraft-Ebbing. The diary teemed with names, big and little, with intricate transactions designed to pad someone's pocket at the expense of someone else, and with the details of assignations, infidelities, promiscuities, and sexual acrobatics of all varieties.

Jake shook his head. "No wonder Riordan was worried."

"He must still be worried," Sheila said.

Jake looked at her thoughtfully. "Yes, of course. The dossier on him is still in limbo."

"Maybe not," Sheila said, thoughtfully.

"That's right," Jake lit a cigarette, and the sound of the flaring match seemed unnaturally loud in the still office. Sheila was right. Riordan might not be worried any more, for the good reason that he could have killed Meed and gotten the incriminating information from the diary.

"But that doesn't explain why he sent the diary to me," he said finally. "Let's stop playing detective and give this thing to Martin."

"You can take care of that errand yourself."

"I wish you'd stop being so damn impersonal," Jake said irritably. "I'm depressed and I'd like to talk with you. Why don't you have dinner with me tonight?"

Sheila shook her head. "Sorry, Jake. Something is bothering you, but you'll have to figure it out for yourself."

"I don't expect you to take me on your lap and calm my fevered crying," Jake said. "I merely want you to have dinner with me and laugh at my gay commentaries on the weather."

"Not tonight," Sheila said. "But thanks."

"Oh, not at all," Jake said drily. He opened the door for her and watched her walk away with quick light steps. . . .

Jake took a cab to Central Station and found Martin sitting in his warm, smoke-filled office, with his feet on his desk, staring out at the swirling snow that was falling over the city.

He put the diary at Martin's elbow and lighted a cigarette while Martin swung himself around in the chair and opened the book. For several moments he skimmed through the pages without comment or expression; and then he glanced up at Jake, and said quietly, "Where'd you get this?"

Jake told him how he had received the diary, and added that he had noticed a number of pages had been cut out, and that there was no mention of Riordan in the diary.

Martin didn't answer for a moment. He stared at the book and turned a few pages idly, a thoughtful frown on his face. Finally he said, "I want you to do me a favor, Jake. Don't tell anybody about bringing me this, will you?"

"You're the boss."

"I want to surprise some people," Martin said. "I don't want anyone to know how it came into my hands. Okay?"

Jake said okay and then spent a half hour talking with Martin, mainly because there was no place in particular that he wanted to go, and nothing in particular he wanted to do. They didn't talk about the two murders that were on their minds. They talked about local politics, about the days when Jake covered a police beat and Martin was in uniform.

When Jake left he was feeling vaguely nostalgic, but he suspected the feeling was cheap, phony and empty. He decided he might just as well be drunk as sentimental, so he told the cab driver who came along to take him to a bar.

CHAPTER ELEVEN

Mᴀʏ was buried the next morning after a pallid, undenominational service in a North Side chapel. There were banks of magnificent floral offerings about the closed coffin, their heavy fragrance blending nicely with the lugubriously solemn organ music and the pale sincerity of the young man who preached the sermon. The young man wore a gray suit with a black vest and he spoke of May as if she were a faithful dog that had been killed by a careless hunter.

Jake walked out after the service and lit a cigarette. He was feeling bad from the effects of his drinking the night before, and the grotesque nature of the funeral service made him feel worse. May had deserved better than that, he thought ruefully.

Someone dropped a hand on his shoulder and when he turned he saw Mike Francesca standing behind him with a sad smile on his face.

"It was too bad, eh, Jake?" Mike said, with a shake of his head.

"Yes, it was too bad," Jake said.

They moved to the curb to avoid the crowd that was coming out of the chapel.

"May was a good friend of mine for many years," Mike said. "We were very close." He shook his head sadly. "Such good friends we were. The police are having no luck finding her murderer, eh?"

Jake smiled. Mike had several police captains on his payroll and if he wanted to know how a police investigation was going he had only to pick up a phone. "They are temporarily baffled," he said, drily.

"Too bad," Mike said, with a heavy sigh. He peered at Jake with his eyes half-closed and smiled gently. "The diary, I understand, has been found. Did you look through it, Jake?"

"Yes, I looked through it, Mike," Jake said evenly. "I didn't see anything about you that was unflattering."

Mike shook his graying head in a gesture of annoyance. "I knew there wouldn't be," he said. "I mean, I wasn't sure, but my first idea was, 'Why, May won't hurt you, Mike. Don't be a fool.' But I couldn't just relax, you know, so I worried about it."

"I don't think you have to worry any more," Jake said, but as he spoke he realized that he had been working on the assumption that the material cut from the diary must have referred to Dan Riordan.

Actually, it could have referred to anyone. He

wondered if Martin realized that.

Mike touched his arm. "Can I drop you somewhere, Jake?"

Jake said he was going downtown and Mike stepped to the curb and glanced down the street. He didn't wave or change expression; he merely indicated by the gesture that he was through talking and a long, black Cadillac halfway down the block pulled away from the curb and shot down the street to come to a smooth stop before them.

"Ah, here we are," he said with a surprised smile. "Get in, Jake. How're you doing with Dan Riordan?"

"Fair enough," Jake said.

"You know, Jake, some time I must have a talk with you about public relations. Could you get the papers to stop calling me a hoodlum?"

"Why in hell do you care what they call you?"

"I tell you, I don't care, myself, Jake, but I got two granddaughters in a convent out West, and I don't think it is nice for them to have me called a hoodlum. Maybe you would call me this week, and we could have a long lunch and talk this over. Eh?"

The car slid to a stop before the Executives' Building as Mike finished talking, so Jake nodded, and said, "Sure thing."

Mike slipped a card into his hand. "My private number," he said. "You give me a ring, eh?"

"Sure," Jake said.

Mike chuckled good-humoredly and climbed back into his car. The driver let out the clutch and the Cadillac rolled deliberately and insolently through a red light, and then turned left past a sign that said NO LEFT TURN and disappeared down the side street. Jake shrugged and walked into the Executives' Building, wondering why he didn't throw Mike's card away.

The receptionist told him that Noble wanted to see him. Jake found Gary seated at his desk, wearing a flamboyant sport jacket and puffing energetically on a cigar.

"What's up?" Jake said.

"Riordan called me yesterday afternoon, said he'd just talked with you and that you'd told him Prior was hot on his trail. That right?"

"That's what Prior told me," Jake said.

"That means we've got to pull his claws. We've got to hit hard and fast, Jake."

"I'm all for that," Jake said.

Noble stood and looked down at Jake with a worried frown. "Jake, I don't like to mention this, because I know you've been trying hard, but you're just not producing for Riordan. Here it is now, four days since we got the account and we haven't even started planning a campaign."

Jake stretched his legs and rested his head against

the back of the chair. He said, "I'm sick of the account, Gary."

"What the devil is wrong with you?" Noble said. "An account is nothing to get sick over. It's business."

"This one is pretty raw. What the hell can we say for Riordan? There's no defense to make, no extenuating factors to introduce. He's a crook."

"That's not for us to say, thank God," Noble said. "Jake, you're just having a touch of spring fever or something. Here, let me fix you a drink."

He brought Jake a tall Scotch and soda and slapped his shoulder. "That should fix you up. You're tired this morning. But we've got to see Riordan this afternoon at his hotel. He called and made the date. So try, Jake, try like hell to dream up something to keep him quiet for a while."

Jake sipped his drink and shrugged. "All right," he said with very little enthusiasm.

After lunch Jake walked to the Blackstone because the day was clear, and the wind off the lake was refreshingly cold. Riordan opened the door in answer to his knock and Jake saw that Noble and Niccolo were already on hand, and that Brian Riordan was lounging on the sofa with a highball in his hand. Sheila was present and that surprised him. He couldn't figure out her interest in the Riordan account. She was sipping a drink and talking with Brian.

There was a general murmur of greeting which

died away as Denise Riordan strolled in through the dining room, wearing a white satin hostess gown and white satin mules. She smiled at Jake and shook her head ruefully. "Hello," she said. "You took me three falls to a finish in the drinking department, I guess."

Riordan glanced at her evenly, and said, "We're going to be busy here, Denise."

"Okay, I just wanted something to keep me company." She made herself a drink from the tray of bottles on the coffee table. Brian Riordan grinned at her and said, "The picture of typical American womanhood. Modestly attired in a white robe with a low bosom and a straight slug of rye in a highball glass."

"Don't you like the picture?" Denise said carelessly.

"I love it," Brian said.

Riordan watched as she walked across the room and out of sight; then he turned to Noble.

"I called you here to find out what the next move is, so let's get to work," he said.

Noble went into the picture feature he had planned for the Riordan family, but Riordan interrupted him with an irritable wave of his hand.

"That's all right, I suppose, but it doesn't seem like a hell of a lot. Who really cares that I carve whaling ships out of corks as a hobby, and water my own front lawn? I want something startling, damn it, something to slow these Federal snoops down to a crawl."

"Well, in that case," Noble said, as confidently as if he knew where the sentence was going to end. "In that case, we'd better do some thinking out loud." He took a cigar from his pocket and unwrapped the tinfoil with the same care a man would use in disarming a land mine. "I have an idea that might be feasible, but I'd rather hear from Jake first," he said.

Jake had been thinking while Noble and Riordan talked. An idea that was just about cheap and unsavory enough to work had occurred to him. It was a lulu, he thought. A real beaut.

"Riordan looked at him. "Well?"

"Yes, I've got something," Jake said. "First of all, and this will be news to you, the police have May's diary."

"How do you know that?" Riordan said.

"I got that much from Lieutenant Martin. Also, and what is more important to us, there's no mention of you in her diary. Maybe there was at one time, but someone has been at work with a scissors and you're out of the star-studded cast."

There was a silence in the room for a moment, and then Riordan said thoughtfully, "That's very interesting."

Brian Riordan looked at his father with a grin. "Damn interesting. Someone else has the dirt on you now." He laughed and slumped down comfortably in the couch. "Perhaps somebody here can help you out. Do any of you happen to have the record of the old man's boyish pranks during the war? He was a cute one, you know, with his self-exploding barrels and stratospheric profits."

Riordan turned to his son, and Jake sensed a finality in the set of his broad shoulders.

"That's all of that, Brian," he said.

"Now don't get tremulous and sensitive," Brian said.

Riordan looked at him calmly for a moment, and there was a curious expression of relief on his face. Then he walked slowly across the floor and stopped before Brian.

"You rotten little fake," he said, enunciating each word with relish. "I've listened to your moral blackmail for the last time."

With a sudden strong gesture he fastened his hand in the lapels of Brian's sport jacket; and then he jerked him powerfully to his feet. Brian's breathing came harder, but he stared into his father's eyes with an insolent smile.

"You came home four years ago," Riordan said in a savage voice. "I provided you with an income that you couldn't earn if you were fifty times as smart as you are, and lived to be a thousand. You squandered it like a brainless fool, and sneered at me for having it to give to you. You made free with everything I owned because you think you've earned it. Well, by

God, I'll show you what you've earned, and what you deserve. From now on you can join the other war heroes and get a job as a bricklayer or a truck driver."

Riordan swung his son around with a twist of his arm, and propelled him toward the door with a mighty shove. Brian staggered backwards and barely kept himself from falling. But he managed a smile as he straightened the lapels of his coat. "You've done something very stupid, you know." He turned and opened the door, and walked out without a backward glance.

Riordan walked over and kicked the door shut. He came back to the center of the room, and said to Jake, "All right, what did you have on your mind?"

Jake had watched the scene between father and son with interest, for there was a nagging feeling in his mind that there was an importance in it greater than a conclusive parental explosion. He felt that it was a lead to something else, but he couldn't get it into place, or evaluate it as part of a design or pattern. What he had seen was an unrelated, self-contained scene; but he thought it would fit significantly into a larger picture if only he could guess where or how.

"All right," Riordan said again. "Did you have something to say?"

Jake said, "Yes, I have," and got his thoughts back in order. The clash between the Riordans had charged the atmosphere with excitement; and Jake waited a

175

moment until the tension eased, until he had everyone's attention. "Here it is," he said. "The police have May's diary, and we know there's nothing in it to incriminate you, Riordan. But there has been plenty of gossip about the diary, and the damaging material it is supposed to contain. Our best bet now is to demand that it be produced and examined."

"I don't get it," Riordan said.

"There's no mystery, or even originality in what I'm suggesting," Jake said. "You need a smoke screen, so we'll blow up a beauty. The smoke screen, if you aren't familiar with the term in public relations, is a device whereby you prove that everybody else is a bastard too. You give your audience someone else to boo, and make a fast exit before the bricks start flying."

Riordan rubbed his jaw thoughtfully. "You've seen the diary, I suppose?"

"No," Jake remembered just in time that Martin had told him not to mention receiving it.

"Then how do you know there's no reference to me in it?"

"Lieutenant Martin told me that much. And I'm guessing May's account is on the torrid side and will drag in dozens of prominent people. That, of course, is what we want."

"What good will smearing a lot of other people do for me?" Riordan said, impatiently.

"Let me demonstrate by example what I mean," Jake said. He lit a cigarette and glanced at Sheila. She met his eyes and smiled. "You surprise even me," she said. "I didn't know you had it in you."

"I'm full of surprises," Jake said, and turned away from her. "Think back, Riordan, to a certain Congressional investigation last year, in which one of our most glamorous industrialists was on the spot. Remember?"

"Yes," Riordan said, looking interested. "I remember it."

"Well, here was the point: The industrialist had built a giant submarine with government money. Some people said the submarine was about as practical as a Rube Goldberg invention. Others said it was all right. The committee wanted to know one way or the other, so they had an investigation. But the damnedest thing happened. The industrialist's bodyguard got on the stand somehow, and began talking about the gala entertaining that had gone on aboard his boss' yacht! The result was that a dozen expensive chippies were called to testify, and they gave the public a Roman festival. They told all about champagne breakfasts and midnight bathing parties at which most of the participants wore nothing but drunken smiles.

"This had nothing much to do with the submarine, of course. But who the hell cared about that, when he could listen to a model tell of being pursued up the rigging of a ship by a drunken satyr? The answer is nobody. The submarine was forgotten. The public had a circus; the committee, I think, had its appropriation cut the next session of Congress.

"Do you understand now? We'll scream for the diary and defy Senator Hampstead and young Prior. We'll go to Washington and drag with us every name mentioned in May's diary."

"A great number of people are going to be hurt," Sheila said.

"That's the beauty of it," Noble said, cheerfully. "You can't tell who's good or bad in a deal like this. Everyone is suspected of being a triple-distilled bastard, and that spreads the guilt around. Riordan, your defective barrels won't have a chance if they're competing with fornication in the upper classes."

"It's okay," Riordan said, with a grin. "I like it. But how can we get the diary made public?"

"We'll see to that," Jake said, and turned to Niccolo. "Dean, get started right away with items to the columns to the effect that the government is going to use May's diary in its case against Riordan. And follow that with items that Riordan is demanding that the diary be produced so that his accusers can be shown up as the lying bastards they are. Maybe tomorrow we can sell the *Trib* an editorial on it."

"You want it pretty strong, eh?" Dean asked. "Outraged citizen fighting the forces of bureaucracy, eh?"

"That's it."

Jake turned from Niccolo and saw that Sheila was looking at him evenly. They faced each other without speaking while Niccolo joined Noble and Riordan for a drink.

"Well," Sheila said, quietly. "You've come up with a master stroke. A real gem. They'll teach this one to kids in public relations classes."

"It's been done before."

"Yes, I'm sure it has. You know, of course, that some innocent people are going to get kicked right in the teeth. And you know who you're doing it for, and what he is."

Jake didn't answer her for a moment. They seemed alone in the room, in a vacuum into which the clatter of glasses and the conversation didn't penetrate. Somehow he seemed far away from her, and the gulf widened each second he remained silent.

Finally he said, "I know what I'm doing, if that's what you mean."

"I wanted to be sure."

"And you're sure now?"

"Yes. Goodbye, Jake."

He watched her walk quickly across the room and out the door; and he knew it was a final exit.

Niccolo came over to him. "One thing, Jake. How do you want me to handle the fact that the diary was sent to you?"

Jake lit a cigarette. "I don't give much of a damn how you handle that point, Dean," he said. He drew deeply on his cigarette and was turning away, when the significance of this question hit him squarely. He turned to Dean and said, "How did you know it was sent to me, Dean?"

"What do you mean?" Dean said.

"Which word don't you understand?" Jake said. "I asked you how you knew the diary was sent to me. No one knew that but Lieutenant Martin. The only other person who knows who received the diary is the person who sent it to me."

Dean grinned and said, "I've got a big mouth, Jake, but don't let it throw you. I got that information from Toni Ryerson."

"Where in hell did she get it?"

"Her office adjoins yours, remember? She saw you open the package and I guess she recognized the diary from the descriptions of it in the newspapers. She told me this morning that she *thought* you'd received the diary. When I heard you say you *knew* the police had it, I assumed she had made a correct guess."

"I see," Jake said. "You startled me for a second. Now what did you want?"

"Well, how shall I handle the fact that the cops have May's diary, and that you gave it to them? I mean, isn't that secret information?"

180

"Just don't mention it, then," Jake said. He shrugged and looked directly at Niccolo. "Actually, I don't care what you do."

"I don't get it," Nicollo said, with a puzzled smile.

"It's not important," Jake said. He stared at the door through which Sheila had left and rubbed a hand tiredly across his forehead. What he'd said to Dean surprised him; it hadn't been deliberate. Yet it expressed perfectly the way he felt about Dean, about Riordan, and about Noble.

The consuming distaste he felt for himself left no room for any interest in anyone else.

He saw himself now as he must have appeared to Sheila; and the view was depressing. The plan he had proposed to Riordan was cheap and ugly; and its execution would require a man of strong stomach and prehensile sensibilities. Himself, in short.

But that was not what nagged him. Business at its best frequently required a dash of knavish skulduggery, and most people played along because they had to, because their livelihood depended on it. But that wasn't the case with him. He had suggested a shoddy plan of action quickly, instinctively and easily. It just came naturally to him.

Noble came over with a drink in his hand, a wide relieved smile on his face. "We're in high gear now, Jake. That idea of yours was terrific. I wish I'd thought of it."

"Yes, I wish you had too," Jake said.

Noble lowered his voice slightly. "Riordan's damned pleased."

"That's good." He looked at the door where Sheila had left, and said, almost as an afterthought, "I'm through, Gary. I'm quitting."

"Quitting?" Noble said. "What do you mean?"

"It's a simple word. You spell it with a 'q' as in 'queasy.'"

"Jake, you're talking like an ass. You can't quit now."

"I'm sorry, Gary. I'm not doing this gracefully, I suppose. But I'm fed up, right to the teeth."

Riordan had come up beside them as Jake was speaking. He looked at Noble and then took the cigar from his mouth. "What's the trouble?" he said. "I heard Jake say he's quitting."

"I heard him, too," Noble said, with a touch of panic in his voice. "But he doesn't mean it."

Riordan looked at Jake and said, "Well, how about it? You serious?"

"Yes, I'm quite serious," Jake said.

"You think we're licked, eh? Is that it?"

"No, that isn't it," Jake said. "I suppose I should explain myself succinctly and graphically. But it seems a big bother."

"Jake, what's got into you?" Noble exploded.

"He's squeamish about working for a thief," Riordan said, with a hard smile.

Jake met Riordan's eyes evenly. "You're putting words in my mouth, but they aren't bad ones. This job stinks to high heaven. So I'm clearing out. Good luck."

He picked up his hat and coat and went to the door.

Riordan said, "High moral attitudes are a luxury, you'll find. Only the very rich can afford them."

Jake paused with his hand on the knob. "I never noticed you displaying any."

Riordan laughed good naturedly. "Of course not. That's how I got rich," he said.

Jake looked at the three men, Niccolo, Noble, and Riordan, all standing with drinks in their hands and regarding him with varying expressions. And it occurred to him then with sudden clearness that he knew a great deal about who had murdered May Laval and Avery Meed.

He smiled and started to answer Riordan; he decided he didn't have the time. Opening the door he waved a goodbye to them and walked briskly to the elevators.

CHAPTER TWELVE

Fifteen minutes later Jake was ringing Sheila's bell. She opened the door and when she saw him she tried to close it; but he put a foot inside and pushed his way into the room.

"Please go away," she said, and he saw that she had been crying. She turned from him and sat down on the sofa before the fire. "I meant it. I want you to go away," she said.

"I've got a little speech to deliver," Jake said. "Can I sit down?"

She didn't answer, and from the set of her shoulders he knew she wouldn't. He sat on the arm of the sofa and removed his hat.

"It's just this," he said. "I know why you divorced me and I know why you're sick of me now. I've changed since we were married. Given a soupçon of encouragement I could be something spectacular in the bastard line. You saw it coming and got out before I reached the stage of dismembering children in a spirit of good clean fun."

"Can't you say it without sounding like a night club entertainer?" Sheila said, fumbling for a cigarette.

Jake held his lighter for her, but she pushed his hand away and used matches from the coffee table.

"I'll try," Jake said quietly. "When I met you I was no prize, admittedly; but I had certain values and certain ideas that I respected. I took people as they came, regardless of their personal, religious, or ethical idiosyncrasies, and I didn't want to see anyone get hurt."

He put a cigarette in his mouth, lit it and inhaled deeply. For a moment he watched Sheila in silence, and then shrugged and continued. "But I changed. I can't blame the public relations business, or anything else, I suppose. But it hit me this afternoon that I was stirring around in a slimy job, and not particularly minding it." He shook his head and tossed his cigarette into the fireplace. "I'm not saying this very well. But I'm fed up. I'm through. I've told Noble that already."

He watched Sheila's still face and the firelight in her hair. He was tired and empty; but it wasn't a bad feeling.

"That's the end of the speech," he said.

"What are you going to do now?" Sheila asked.

"I'm going to tell Martin some things about a couple of murders. After that I'm going to send you a dozen roses and go on relief."

Sheila raised her head slowly and he saw that she

was crying and making no attempt to check the tears.

"Can't you do something about this middle-class emotion?" he said uncomfortably.

"Give me a hanky."

He gave her his handkerchief. "I'm sorry," she said. Then she shook her head. "No, I'm not. I waited for it two years and it doesn't matter a damn bit that I'm behaving like a fool."

Jake sat beside her. "Then, in the traditional phrase, it isn't too late?"

Sheila put her hand against his cheek. "The time wasn't important. I just wanted you to wake up, I suppose I'd have waited until I was an old hag for that to happen. Maybe I shouldn't say that, it's not good politics. But it's the way I feel, Jake. I love you, you know."

Jake had no urge to be flippant. He simply felt very lucky. "Why didn't you just tell me what you wanted?" he said.

"That wouldn't have been any good. You had to see it yourself and make your own decision, one way or the other. I thought if I left, you might wake up. Anyway, I couldn't bear to be around and watch you changing into a person I didn't know and didn't like."

Jake put his hands on her shoulders and pulled her close to him, and for a moment they didn't do any more talking; then Sheila pushed him away. "That can wait. Right now I want to know what you meant

187

when you said you were going to tell Martin about a couple of murders."

"I dislike easily distracted women," Jake said, and then his mood changed and he sighed. "This is hardly the time for the light touch. I've stumbled onto a number of things in the past couple of days. They add up to a pretty good guess as to who killed whom. But I can't fit Niccolo into the picture."

"Niccolo?" Sheila asked.

"You couldn't know about that, I guess. Well, here it is: This afternoon Niccolo asked me how to handle the angle that May's diary had been sent to me. Well, he couldn't have known that I received the diary unless he sent it to me."

"Did you ask him about it?"

"Yes. And he had a nice glib story. He said that Toni Ryerson was sitting at her desk when I unwrapped the diary. She recognized it from the newspaper descriptions, and told Niccolo."

"Well, that's logical enough."

"No, it isn't," Jake said. "Toni's desk and mine are not in line, Sheila. Sitting at her desk, she couldn't see what I was doing at my desk."

"Are you sure?" Sheila asked.

"Pretty sure," Jake said. "But I'm not going to guess about it."

"What do you mean?"

"We're going down to the office and check. You see what it means if Niccolo is lying, don't you?"

"I get it all right," Sheila said.

She came out of her bedroom five minutes later with fresh makeup on, and her hair tucked under the rim of a small woolen hat.

"I hurried," she said.

"It doesn't show. You look perfect."

"You sound normal again. Cheerful, I mean." She smiled and took his arm. "It's a nice change."

Outside snow was falling and darkness had settled thickly and suddenly. They waited on the curb of Lake Shore Drive for a Loop-bound cab while in the opposite lanes four rows of traffic flowed smoothly away from the city, their headlights cutting clear tunnels into the night.

Jake thought about Sheila's comment with a slightly cynical smile. Yes, he had made a change of a sort, and he did feel better. The depression that had affected him for the past days was gone, and he guessed that it had stemmed from a subconscious realization that his work for Riordan was hitting a new low in his career with Gary Noble.

Things were not only bleak, they were confusing. It was curious, he thought, that moral rehabilitation should generally be accompanied by the renunciation of money, in one way or another. In fact, it was about the only way of proving the purity of your desire to be a better man. Yet the world respected the making of money as it respected nothing else, in spite of the academic maxims that two could live as cheaply as one, that the best things in life were free, and that the rich were really a collection of miserable neurotics.

You came to realize very quickly that the best things in life were not only not free, but were usually the most expensive things in life; and that the rich, far from being miserable neurotics, were pleasant, contented people who led charming, satisfying lives. And so you worked to make some money but in the process became a fouled-up moral cripple. It was all very confusing.

The thing was, Jake decided, that he probably was made to be a poor newspaperman, instead of a rich philosopher. At any rate, he realized, the days ahead would not be rosy sequences from a grade B picture.

But he wasn't worried too much about it now.

He was worried about murder. He had a conviction that he could explain the bewildering and violent events that had begun with the murder of May Laval. However, a conviction wasn't enough. He had to marshal his guesses into a concrete, unassailable pattern of evidence; he had to put his conviction into an equation that would solve the identity of a clever murderer. Or possibly two.

That was enough to worry about at the moment.

The reception room of the agency was darkened, and the thick carpet muffled their footsteps as they walked across the floor and into the corridor that led to Jake's office. From where they stood they saw a narrow beam of light coming from the open door of the art department; but they heard no sound and the floor was apparently deserted.

"I'm scared," Sheila said. Her voice was matter-of-fact, but Jake felt her hand tighten on his arm.

"Don't feel superior about it," he said. "So am I. Let's go."

They walked down the dark corridor, keeping close together and unconsciously moving quietly and cautiously.

Inside his office Jake snapped on the overhead lights, and then walked into Toni's office and did the same.

He went behind Toni's desk and looked through the open door to his own office. Sheila said, "She could see your desk, all right. Maybe Niccolo wasn't lying, Jake."

"Something's wrong," Jake said. "Look, sit down in Toni's chair and put your feet on the desk."

"What's your idea?"

"I'm not sure."

He went into his office and sat behind the desk. Sheila called out from Toni's office, "Okay, I'm set."

Jake turned his head and saw Sheila's slim ankles

crossed on the top of Toni's desk. She was wearing black suède pumps with tiny bows over the instep. He could also see her knees where the skirt had pulled up.

He stood up and walked back to Toni's office. Sheila said, "What's wrong, Jake?"

"Somebody is lying, if only on a technicality," he said. He lit a cigarette with an automatic gesture. "I've used that office for two years and I know what I'm likely to see when I look around. One of the familiar sights was Toni's ankles. But that was all I saw. Now under the same circumstances I get a view of your legs that is quite a bit more revealing."

Sheila came around to his side. "What does it mean, though?"

Jake didn't answer her; instead he got down on his knees and inspected the legs of the desk. And he found what he had expected to find. The depressions made in the carpet by the legs of the desk were clearly visible; and they were about a foot behind the present position of the desk's legs.

"Somebody moved the desk forward enough to make Niccolo's story check," he said.

"Who?" Sheila asked.

Jake sighed and shook his head. "Hard to say. Let's review the facts. Niccolo made a compromising statement to me this afternoon. He indicated that he knew I'd received the diary. Logically, the only person

192

who would know that would be the person who sent it to me. Right?"

"I knew you received the diary," Sheila said. "Don't forget that, Jake."

"I'm passing you by for the moment," he said. "Getting back to the facts; Niccolo had a plausible explanation for his information. Toni told him about it, he said. However, he said she saw me while she was sitting at her desk. That's impossible. However, it now appears that such a thing is possible, because Toni's desk was moved, and its present position makes Niccolo's story a thing of pristine beauty."

"What are you going to do?"

"We're going calling," Jake said. "I've always wanted to see Toni in her native environment. This seems like a good chance. Come on."

Toni Ryerson lived on the near North Side in the fifteen hundred block of Clark Street. The neighborhood had been deteriorating for decades but the progress had been halted, or rather rerouted, during the war, by an influx of single girls who had come from smaller cities to work in Chicago; and by the colony of homosexuals, artists, writers, and draft evaders, which had sprung up in the area at the same time, apparently attracted by its flavor of *fin de siècle* decay, and the low rent. Now the district boasted a number of studios with slanted windows blinking toward the north, and pizzeria bars and sidewalk cafés.

Jake paid off their cab and stepped out into the snow before Toni's address, a three story brownstone apartment building.

"Why should she live in a place like this?" Sheila asked as they went up to the entrance.

"Who knows?" Jake shrugged, looking for Toni's name in the hallway. "She probably thinks it's a slice of raw, pulsing life, and she wants to do a little pulsing. Actually she wants a suburban home with an incinerator and mortgage, and a husband who cheats on her at American Legion conventions."

"Ah, bitter," Sheila sighed. "Do you really believe you can figure out human motivations so accurately?"

Jake found Toni's name halfway down the metal rack and punched the adjacent button. Then he smiled at Sheila. "In a word, no. I don't know what Toni wants, or anybody else, for that matter. I was guessing, and indulging my craving for epigrammatic inanities." He kissed her hard and quickly on the mouth. "I know what I want, however."

The buzzer sounded; and Jake pushed open the door and followed Sheila up the uncarpeted steps. A door opened above them and Toni's voice called, "Who is it?"

Jake said, "Jake and Sheila. Can we see you a minute?"

"Why, sure," Toni said cheerfully.

She waited for them on the third floor landing. They

194

exchanged hellos and followed Toni into her one-room apartment, where Stravinsky was coming from a record player and one glaring, unshaded bulb hung from the ceiling.

"How about a drink?" Toni said.

"Jake said, "No thanks. I want to talk to you a moment."

"Why, sure," Toni said again. She looked puzzled. "Let's sit down, anyway."

There were several wooden chairs in the room, surrounding an immense table on which a portable typewriter was almost lost in a clutter of books and manuscript.

Toni pulled a chair from the table and sat down, with her legs crossed, tailor fashion.

Jake sat on the edge of her work table. "Here's the reason for the visit, Toni,'" he said. "Yesterday some-body sent me May Laval's diary. Niccolo has told me that you were at your desk when I got it, and recog-nized the diary from the descriptions of it in the papers. Is that right?"

Toni looked guilty. "Yes, I saw it, Jake."

"And you told Niccolo about it?"

"I—I didn't know I was doing wrong. I've just got a big mouth, I guess."

"There's no reason you shouldn't have told Dean about it," Jake said. "It was just one of those things, and you had a perfect right to mention it to anyone."

"You're making me feel a little better," Toni said. "I thought you were going to tell me I'm a snooping little brat."

"Perish the thought," Jake said. "I'm not going to tell you anything like that. However, I'm going to tell you that you're a stupid little liar, Toni."

"What do you mean?" she cried.

"When did you move your desk?" Jake said evenly.

"I didn't—I don't know when I moved it," Toni said, twisting her hands together.

Jake lit a cigarette, and said mildly, "You love Dean, I suppose."

"Yes."

"You'd like to keep him from getting hurt, then?"

Toni's eyes became enormous. "Yes," she whispered.

"All right, just relax a little bit and listen to me. You can't see my desk from your desk. You couldn't, at least, until yesterday or today. Now, your desk has been moved forward to a spot where it's in line with mine. Coincidentally enough, that move corroborates the story about the diary that Niccolo told me. Curious, isn't it?"

Toni wet her lips. "I—I don't know."

"Dean's in trouble. Serious trouble. You aren't doing him any service by keeping quiet now. Let's have the story."

Toni looked to Sheila, then back at Jake. "Dean called me yesterday afternoon," she said, in a low, hesitant voice. "He asked me to tell you I'd seen you get the diary."

"What time was that?"

"I don't know. He was at Mr. Riordan's apartment, though."

Jake thought that Niccolo hadn't wasted any time correcting his slip about the diary.

"Go on," Jake said.

"Dean sounded upset," Toni said. "He said if you asked me had I seen you get the diary that I was to say yes. And I was also to tell you that I'd told him about it. Then he asked me if I could see your desk when I was sitting at my own. I said no. For a few seconds he didn't say anything. Then he told me to move my desk up enough so that it was in line with yours."

"And you did, of course?"

"Yes."

"Anything else?"

"No. I asked him why he wanted me to lie for him, but he just said, 'Why not?' and hung up."

Jake said to Toni, "Do you have a phone?"

Surprisingly, she had. It was on a piano stool in the closet. Jake picked up the receiver and gave the operator Niccolo's number. Toni was beginning to cry. "He'll hate me," she said.

"I don't think so," Jake said.

The phone on the other end was lifted. Jake's hand

tightened on the receiver.

"Yes?" It was Niccolo's voice, low and guarded.

"Dean, this is Jake."

There was silence. Then Niccolo said, "What's on your mind?"

"I'm at Toni's. Let's don't waste time. She told me the whole story."

Dean was silent, and Jake said, "Are you still there?"

"I didn't bolt for the door," Niccolo said. His voice was tired. "Where are you now?"

"At Toni's."

"Well, do me a favor. I shouldn't have dragged her into this mess, but I was desperate. Tell her for me she's a good kid, and that I'm sorry. Will you do that?"

"I'll do that," Jake said. "Now let's come to the point. How did you know I received May's diary?"

"I sent it to you," Niccolo said. "I wrapped it with brown paper, put your name on it, and dropped it into a mail box. That's how I knew you got it, Jake."

Jake felt perspiration starting on his forehead. He said, "Where did you get it, Dean?"

"I got it from Avery Meed, Riordan's little batman. I killed Meed, Jake. I killed him and took the diary. Does that shock you?"

"You're crazy. Don't talk any more. I'll come over and we'll go over this thing. Will you wait there for me, Dean?"

"Sorry, Jake. Thanks, but I have other plans. I need

a half hour's start. How about a half hour for auld lang syne? Have a drink, smoke a couple of cigarettes before you call the police, eh, Jake?"

"I won't give you thirty seconds unless you listen to me. Why in hell did you do it, Dean?"

Niccolo chuckled, and Jake could imagine the light in his eye and the cynical good humor of his strong and handsome face. "I have a sordid story in the balcony, doctor," Niccolo said. "Jake, I killed Meed because I'm a smart operator."

"Stop this neurotic babbling," Jake said sharply. "Give me the story."

Toni had come closer to the phone. "He's in trouble, isn't he?" she said in an anguished whisper. Sheila put an arm around her shoulder and held her close.

"Okay," Niccolo said, quietly. "I'll give it to you, Jake. But in exchange for that half hour. Is it a deal?"

"Go ahead."

"Here it is then, in my own clean and sparkling style. I needed money, Jake. I liked the horses but they didn't like me, Mr. Bones. I got in deep with some characters who weren't interested in excuses or good intentions. Remember our first conference with Riordan? He said that May Laval had some dope on him. I was in a straw-grabbing mood, so I decided to see May. I hoped to talk her into joining me in a deal to pry Riordan loose from some of his cash. Blackmail is the traditional word, I guess." Niccolo laughed drily. "Still interested?"

"Yes."

"Fine. I went to May's the morning she was murdered. But I was too late. A little man, whom I later learned was Avery Meed, was going up the steps of her house. He went in and came out not more than a minute later, with a flat book under his arm. I didn't get the pitch. Anyway, I lost my nerve. I went home, but the next morning I met Meed in your office. By that time I knew that May had been murdered, and that the diary was missing. So I reasoned that Meed had killed May and taken the diary. The rest was pretty simple. I followed him when he left the office —you wanted me that morning but I was gone, remember? Anyway, I talked to Meed in his apartment. He had an appointment with Riordan and he didn't have much time. Neither did I, Jake. I told him what I knew, and gave him an opportunity to join my little deal. But he turned me down. More than that, he reached for a phone to call the police. He must have been bluffing, but I couldn't take a chance. I killed him and took the diary. Later that morning, I clipped the information in it that pertained to Riordan, and sent the rest of the diary to you."

"Do you still have the dope on Riordan?"

"Yes," Niccolo said, and laughed. "It's plenty hot, Jake. But it didn't do me any good. I sent you the diary because I hoped you'd tell Riordan. I thought it might put a little psychological pressure on him to know that the dirt had gotten into someone else's hands. But I'm a bad guesser. I called Riordan the next night and made him a proposition. He told me to go to hell and hung up. And that's just half of it. Tonight I called that character Prior, the government man. I offered him the dope on Riordan for a price, and he told me to go to hell, too. Funny, isn't it?"

"Dean, you can't help yourself by running now. You'd better face this thing."

"You promised me a half hour, remember?"

"You'll get the half hour," Jake said.

"Okay. We'll see how far I can get. I have plans but I don't honestly expect them to work. I'm kind of disappointed in myself, Jake. Take it easy."

The phone clicked in Jake's ear. He jiggled the hook automatically; then he shrugged and put the receiver back into place.

"What did he do?" Toni whispered.

Jake looked at her for a moment without speaking. Then he said, "He killed Avery Meed."

Toni frowned as if the words had no meaning for her, and then she sat down in a straight chair and began to rub her forehead. "That's not—Dean couldn't do that," she said, in a puzzled, reasonable voice, and started to cry. The tears ran down her cheeks, but she stared at the opposite wall, sitting straight in the chair, and made no attempt to brush them away.

Sheila came to Jake's side and he put his arm around her shoulder. "He wants me to wait half an hour before calling the police," he said.

"I see. Do you have a cigarette?"

They lit cigarettes and Jake glanced at his watch. "Damn it," he said.

Fifteen minutes passed. Toni had stopped crying. She stared at Jake now in a beseeching silence, as if begging him to tell her nothing was wrong.

The half hour passed.

Jake picked up the phone and called the police board. He asked for Homicide. The sergeant on duty switched his call to Lieutenant Martin's office.

"Yes?" Martin said crisply.

"This is Jake. I've got some news for you."

"Fine. What is it?"

Jake heard Toni crying again, and he let out his breath wearily. "I've got the man who killed Avery Meed. All wrapped up in a fancy package."

"Who've you got?" Martin said, his voice quickening with interest.

"Dean Niccolo."

Martin was silent for several seconds. Then he said, in a thoughtful voice, "That's funny, Jake. Dean Niccolo was murdered in his apartment about fifteen minutes ago. We're just going out there."

CHAPTER THIRTEEN

Jake left Sheila with Toni and caught a cab for the North Side. He knew the patrolman who was standing inside the lobby of Niccolo's building. He told him that Martin was expecting him and went up to the third floor landing, where the Lieutenant was talking with a detective from the district.

They nodded to each other and Martin led him into Niccolo's apartment.

Niccolo's tweed-clad body lay on a grass rug in the center of the large, high-ceilinged living room. His face was buried in the crook of his arm, and except for the blood on his cheek he might have been asleep. The blood came from a wound in his temple and had stained his thick black hair.

"It was at close range," Martin said. "Probably a .32. Now what was this about his killing Meed?"

Jake looked away from Dean's huddled figure. "That was his story," he said. "He made a slip, you see, talking with me about the diary. He said something that indicated he knew I'd received it. When I called him on it, he gave me a song-and-dance about getting the information from Toni Ryerson, whose office adjoins mine."

Martin held up a hand irritably. "Let's go slow, Jake. You seem to be running over with information."

"Okay," Jake said. He started again and told Martin every detail of his conversation with Dean Niccolo, and of his interview with Toni Ryerson, and Dean's original mistake. When he finished Martin scowled and ran a hand abstractedly through his thinning brown hair.

"So he killed Meed, eh? That leaves May and himself for us to figure out, doesn't it?"

Without waiting for an answer he drifted away and began talking with a detective who was dusting the arms of the light maple chairs for prints.

Jake glanced around the smartly furnished room, noting the monk's cloth drapes, the modern drawings, the liquor cabinet and shelves of records. Niccolo had enjoyed the good things of life. Several of the pictures had been pulled down from the wall, he noticed, and the drawers of a small desk had been removed and their contents dumped on the floor.

Martin walked back to Jake, massaging the bridge of his nose thoughtfully, and Jake said, "Did your men make the search here?"

"No. This is just the way we found it. Someone made a quick search after letting him have it, I'd say."

"Any ideas?" Jake said.

"No, I wouldn't go that far," Martin said drily. He looked at Jake with an odd expression. "You got any ideas?"

"As a matter of fact, yes," Jake said. "Supposing Avery Meed killed May to get the diary? Logical?"

"Reasonably so. We've found Meed's prints on the table where May kept the diary. He had a motive, opportunity, and so forth. Yeah, it's logical."

"How about those double crosses drawn on the mirror with lipstick and the clothes of May's that were strewn about, and so forth? Do you think Meed did all that?"

Martin smiled slowly and touched Jake's tie with his forefinger. "That's a nice tie. I wouldn't have thought green would go with gray that well. But to answer your question: You said Niccolo said he was outside May's when Meed went in. Well, according to Niccolo, Meed was only inside a minute. That wouldn't have given him time to talk the deal over with May, murder her, tear up her clothes, draw on the mirror with lipstick, and so forth. That would take ten or fifteen minutes." Martin lit a cigarette deliberately and blew smoke at the ceiling. "Maybe Niccolo was wrong about the time?"

"I'm betting he wasn't," Jake said. "Niccolo had been in radio quite a while before coming with us. He could look at a page of copy and tell how long it would take to read it over the air. I'd say he'd make a good witness."

"You're saying that Meed didn't murder May. That he couldn't possibly have."

"No, you're saying that," Jake said.

A flicker of annoyance crossed Martin's face and he said, sardonically, "How long are you going to keep me in suspense, Jake? Do you know anything I can use?"

"I honestly don't know," Jake said. "I'll try though. Do you know that Riordan's wife, Denise, and young Brian have been two-timing the old man with gay indifference, so to speak?"

"I've known that from the start," Martin said.

Jake shrugged. "Well, you're ahead of me."

"I know that Dan Riordan didn't spend the night of May's murder in Gary," Martin said. "I know a helluva lot, Jake. I know that your boss, Gary Noble, has lied to me about what he did the night of the murder. I wonder if anyone is telling the truth."

"How about Mike Francesca?" Jake said, with a smile.

"I know all about Mike Francesca," Martin snapped. He dropped his cigarette and put his foot on it heavily; and then he looked at Jake with embarrassment. "I'm sorry," he said. "I can't make things add up in this case. It's got me edgy."

A uniformed patrolman who had been going

through a shelf of books came over to Martin with an envelope in his hand. "I just found this behind a row of books, Lieutenant."

Martin took the envelope from him, opened it and removed a sheaf of clippings. He opened them and Jake saw that they were covered with May's back-slanted script.

"This is damn interesting," Martin said.

The clippings were obviously those that had been cut from May's diary and Jake, as he read over Martin's shoulder, saw why Riordan had been worried.

The clippings contained the story of his wartime jugglings, not in elaborate detail, but in implications, scraps of conversations, and forthright opinions by May of Riordan's activities. There were facts, figures and dates, all adding up to a pretty clear picture of how Riordan had cheated the government through the substitution of cheap grade steel, and of how he had bribed the inspector, Nickerson, to okay the faulty barrels.

"Looks like this Riordan is quite a bastard," Martin said, and looked at Jake coldly. "You enjoy working for him?"

"I didn't, so I quit," Jake said.

"Well," Martin said and cleared his throat noisily. "I seem to make an ass out of myself every time I get away from murders."

"Forget it," Jake said. "Does this information give

you a lead?"

"An obvious one. Who would want this information hushed up? Riordan."

"Tell me this," Jake said. "Did you ever find any additional diary of May's?"

"Now you're getting smart. That was the first thing I looked for when she was murdered. You see, the diary we recovered ran up until the end of 1948, and this is more than a year later. People usually don't give up the diary habit once they start. When they do it's a lead-pipe cinch they wouldn't stop on the last day of the year. That's psychology, in case you're wondering how I know. New Year's Day is the time to start a diary because it's an exciting day, it's a fresh start in life. So when I saw that her diary ended on December 31, 1948, I made a little bet that we'd find some further record of her day-to-day routine."

"Well, did you?" Jake said impatiently.

"Oh, yes," Martin said. He lit a cigarette and said casually, "Yes, we found it, all right. May had stopped keeping a written diary at the end of 1948. From then on she had her material typed by an outfit called Autowrite. We found a bundle of typewritten pages in her bedroom, hidden away in a little closet behind her shoe rack."

"What do you mean she had her material typed?" Jake said. "Did she use a secretary?"

"No, a Dictaphone. And it was empty when we

arrived. Either she hadn't been working or the cylinder had been taken away."

Martin excused himself to talk with a district sergeant and Jake wandered to the window and stared down into the snow-blurred street. Everything was coming into shape now, the pattern was taking form. He stood at the window for perhaps three or four minutes, smoking a cigarette, and then he turned and went back to Martin.

"I've got an idea," he said. "Lend me one of your men for a half hour or so, and I may surprise you."

"You haven't asked if there was anything interesting in May's new diary?" Martin said.

"I know damn well there wasn't," Jake said.

"I'm going to arrest Riordan," Martin said. "Does that interest you?"

"Yes and no. Well?"

Martin nodded to a detective from Homicide, a man named Murphy. "Go along with Jake, Murph. He may need some help. When you're through with him check back to Headquarters."

"I'll see you in an hour," Jake said.

"You're going to miss the show," Martin said.

"Maybe not," Jake said. "Come on, Murph."

Downstairs Murphy crawled into his car and said, "Where to, Jake?"

"Find a drugstore, first, I've got to make a call."

Leaving Murphy in the car Jake went into the

warm, sweetly-scented drugstore and walked to the telephone booths. He picked up the city directory and leafed quickly through to the S's, and then slowed down as he searched for the name of May's maid, Ada Swenson. Jake wasn't sure she had a phone. If not, they'd have to make the trip to her home. But she was listed in the book, to his relief.

Then as he dialed her number he went quickly back over the chain of reasoning that had led him to her. He might have slipped, but he couldn't see where or how.

First May was using a Dictaphone. He shouldn't have needed Martin to tell him that. She had said she was going to work the night he had seen her for the last time, and she had said there were no servants in the house at night, because she didn't like them *eavesdropping* on her. If she had been using a typewriter or pen or pencil she wouldn't have had that worry. Therefore she was dictating. That much was fine. But she had intended to work that night—yet the police had not found a cylinder in her Dictaphone.

There could be several explanations for that, of course, the most obvious being that she had decided not to work after all. However, if she had worked, there should have been a dictaphone cylinder in her machine the next morning, unless—it had been taken away by her murderer, or had been mailed away by the maid, Ada Swenson. The woman had told Martin she had mailed a package before discovering May's body.

That last alternative had all of Jake's hopes pinned to it. That "package" had to be the dictaphone cylinder.

He tried to keep his excitement in check as he waited for her phone to answer. There was a chance she'd left town. She could have been in an accident.

"Hello?"

Jake recognized her soft, anxious voice. "Miss Swenson, this is Lieutenant Martin," he said. "Can I talk to you a moment?"

"Why—yes."

"I'd like you to tell me again what you did the morning of Miss Laval's murder. Everything, please."

"Oh, it was terrible," Miss Swenson said, her voice rising. "She was laying on the bed, and I said, 'Good morning' and she didn't answer, and she was dead all the time, and the police came and found her throat had been strangled, and I—"

"Now don't upset yourself, Miss Swenson," Jake said. "What did you do when you entered the house? Immediately after you unlocked the door, what did you do?"

"I closed it," Miss Swenson said.

"Yes. And then what?"

"Oh!" Miss Swenson cried. "I forget. I forget the mail. I took the mail out and then came back and found her there."

Jake's hand tightened on the receiver. "What was it you mailed, Miss Swenson?"

"Like always. First thing she want me to take out the little package and drop it in the box. She left it for me at night, and I mail it in the mail box. Sometimes she leave two or three, but they should go out first, before the dusting. Always Special Delivery."

Jake let out his breath slowly. "Thanks, Miss Swenson, thanks very much," he said.

"Good night. And do you know will anybody else want to know about this? I am leaving soon for sister's, but with you and the other fellow calling me maybe I should plan to leave not right away."

"Did someone else call you about this?" Jake said.

"Oh, yes. Not an hour ago. He wanted to know just like you what I did and about the mail. I almost forgot about the mail to him too, I'm so nervous."

"Who was it called?" Jake said.

"I don't know."

"Well, I don't think you'll be bothered again to-night," Jake said. He replaced the receiver and stared at it for a moment; someone else was thinking along the same line that he was, and that "someone" now knew as much as he did.

He flipped quickly through the phone book again, found the address he wanted and rejoined Murphy in the car. "We're going downtown," he said. "The

Science Building at Wabash and Lake Streets."

The revolving door of the Science Building was locked but Murphy hammered on the glass until he roused the janitor, a shuffling old man with gray hair and filmy blue eyes.

Murphy showed his badge to the janitor through the glass and they were admitted. Jake asked what floor the Autowrite Company was on, and the janitor said the thirteenth.

"Let's go up," Jake said.

The Autowrite Company occupied a three-room suite with an entrance several doors down from the elevators. Murphy told the janitor to unlock the door and Jake walked into the office and snapped on the lights, while Murphy watched him curiously.

Jake went to the filing cabinets and looked through the index for May's account with the company. He found a card with her name on it, listing the dates when recordings were received and when the typed material was returned to her. The last entry showing the receipt of a recording was the day after May's murder. There was no record that the material had been returned, and Jake began to feel excited. He was still on the right track, so far.

There remained now the job of finding the cylinder that contained May's record of what happened the last night she was alive.

There were three desks in the outer office, and on

each there was a wire basket filled with the black dictaphone cylinders.

Jake beckoned to Murphy. "You can give me a hand here. I'm looking for a recording made by May Laval." He picked up a cylinder from the desk and saw that it had a tag attached to it, and on the tag a printed name. "Her name will be on the one we want." He put the first cylinder aside, and started through the pile, while Murphy applied himself with an impressive disinterest to the stack on the middle desk.

The janitor watched them with gloomy suspicion.

Murphy found the recording.

Jake grabbed it eagerly and slipped it into the player alongside the desk, put the phones to his ears, and flicked the switch to start the machine. . . .

He listened for two minutes, and then he said, "Well, I'll be damned," in an astonished voice. And yet he wasn't surprised.

"What's up?" Murphy asked.

Jake took the phones from his ears and removed the cylinder from the player. "There's no time to go into it now, Murph. But here's what I want you to do. I need this recording and a portable dictaphone at Riordan's suite in the Blackstone Hotel in about an hour. Can you handle that?"

"Yeah, we've got a couple of portables at Headquarters. You want one of them, and this cylinder, too?"

214

"Yes, and for God's sake don't let anything happen to the record."

"I'll take care of it," Murphy said laconically, and dropped it into his outside coat pocket.

"Hey!" the janitor said. "You can't take things out of here."

"I'll leave a receipt," Jake said, and sat down at a typewriter. He rattled one off and signed Lieutenant Martin's name to it with a flourish.

"Well, that's different," the janitor said.

Murphy drove Jake down to the Blackstone. The traffic going south was light and they made excellent time. The snow had changed to rain now, a heavy slanting rain that blurred the windshield and haloed street lights with a misty corona. Murphy dropped Jake at the hotel and drove on to Headquarters to get the portable dictaphone.

There was a crowd under the marquee waiting for cabs, and the rain-coated doorman was in the street, blowing his whistle at passing cabs with pointless optimism.

Jake elbowed his way through the press of people and trotted up the steps to the lobby. He started for the elevators but saw Martin and Gregory Prior standing at the desk talking to the room clerk. Changing directions he came up behind them and tapped Martin on the shoulder.

Martin turned, and his face was hard. "We're too late. Riordan checked out an hour ago. The clerk tells us he had a ticket on the TWA flight to the coast."

"What flight?"

"The ten thirty-five. We can catch him at the airport."

Prior nodded to Jake. "I've got a car outside," he said to Martin. Prior was hatless and there were drops of rain in his close-cropped hair. "I've got an interest in Riordan, too, you know."

"Well, let's go," Martin said. "We can both take a crack at him, but not until we get him."

They started for the door and Jake had to hurry to keep up with Martin's long, determined strides. They pushed through the revolving door as a cab pulled up at the hotel.

The occupant struggled through the cluster of people trying to engage the cab; and Jake saw that it was Sheila.

"I hoped you'd be here," she said. "I gave Toni a sleeping powder and she's all right. What's going on?"

Prior cleared his throat. "We've got to hurry."

Jake said to Martin, "Can I bring her along?"

"Sure, bring her along," Martin said.

Prior's car was halfway down the block. They were soaking wet when they climbed in, Jake and Sheila in the rear, Martin and Prior up front. Prior drove down Wabash, then over to Roosevelt Boulevard to Archer

Avenue, the diagonal artery leading to Municipal Airport.

"What's going on?" Sheila said.

"Dan Riordan has flown the coop. Wasn't that a damn foolish thing for him to do, Prior?"

"He knew we had him," Prior said, rubbing a gloved hand over the windshield and leaning forward over the wheel for better visibility. "Possibly he figured he'd be better off trying to get out of the country with as much cash as he could raise. He might manage to stay at liberty quite some time, say in South America."

Prior drove expertly. They reached the airport at ten thirty-four.

Martin was out of the car before Prior brought it to a complete stop.

There was a restless stir of movement in the large, brightly-lighted waiting room, as passengers streamed out the doors leading to the field, and red caps trundled luggage after them in four-wheeled trucks. The monotonous, weary voice of the announcer describing flights and weather in other sections of the country lent a charged excitement to the atmosphere.

Martin made straight for the TWA information desk.

"The ten thirty-five is ready to take off now, sir," the clerk said, answering his question. "I'm afraid you're late."

Martin drew his wallet and showed the clerk his

badge. "We may have to hold that flight," he said.

"Oh." The clerk raised his eyebrows. "I'll try to contact the dispatcher. Will you need any help?"

"I don't think so," Martin said.

Prior came in, spotted them and hurried over. "Everything okay?"

Martin nodded. "Let's go."

He led the way to the field with Prior and Jake at his side. Outside the night was changed to brilliant whiteness by the rows of beacons lining the runway.

Prior suddenly grabbed Martin's arm. "Look." They all stopped and watched the gleaming, four-engined plane that was hurtling down the runway. It drove into the opaque mist of rain and finally cleared the ground and faded almost imperceptibly into the horizon, its blinking wing lights flashing like fireflies in the dark.

"Well," Jake said. "That was a nice exit."

"He won't get far," Martin said. "He should know that."

They drove back to the Loop after Martin had dispatched a wire to police in Kansas City asking them to take Riordan into custody. Martin said he wanted them to come with him to Riordan's apartment.

"What kind of a warrant do you have for him?" he asked Prior a little later.

"We don't have a warrant yet and we don't need one, unless he refuses to cooperate. First, he'll have a hearing before the committee, which has the authority to subpoena any persons or records it requires."

"You're pretty sure of your case?"

"I'd rather wait a bit, but the Senator has the bit in his teeth."

No one talked for a while after that and they drove toward the city with nothing but the lashing rain and wind against the car to break the silence.

Finally Prior said, "Why do you want to go back to Riordan's apartment?"

"There are still some odds and ends," Martin said. He lit a cigarette and looked out the window at the dreary rain, and no one said anything else.

When they reached the Blackstone, Martin said to Prior, "Take Sheila into the lobby and wait for us, will you? I want to talk to Jake a second."

"All right."

"Alone at last," Jake said, as Prior and Sheila ran across the sidewalk and up the steps to the lobby. "What's on your mind?"

Martin turned and rested his arm on the back of the front seat. He drew on his cigarette and the tiny flare of light revealed the smile on his face.

"What did you find at the Autowrite place?" he said mildly.

Jake was reaching for a cigarette but his hand stopped in mid air. "You son of a bitch," he grinned. "You made an errand boy out of me."

"Yeah, that's right. I knew what you were thinking, so I saved myself the trip. You see, there were only three things could have happened to May's last record. One, it would be in her home. Two, the murderer would take it with him. Three, it would be at the Auto-write place getting typed."

"You called Miss Swenson, then?"

"Sure. I knew you would too, and that you'd go down there and look around. No point in both of us working," he said drily.

"You want to hear about it?"

"Not particularly," Martin said, and he was smiling again. "Let's go in and wind this up, Jake."

"Hey, wait a minute," Jake said. "I just have a wonderful theory."

Martin laughed and got out of the car. Jake climbed out and caught his arm. "I'm not going to make accusations that won't stick."

"Look at it this way," Martin said. "I don't have a case either. And I can't open up until I'm dead sure of myself. If these were punks I wouldn't care. But this is a different class of people. You can get things rolling in an unofficial capacity, and when the fireworks start I'll be right there."

"With a pair of handcuffs for me?"

"We have to force this thing," Martin said. "I'm asking a lot, Jake. I know how you've been thinking, and where it's led you. Our theories may support one another. If you'll start things rolling we can wind this up tonight."

"All right," Jake said. "Anything to get out of this damned rain."

CHAPTER FOURTEEN

THE policeman who met them at the door of the Riordan suite made a warning gesture with his hands. Jake looked past him and saw Denise Riordan sitting in an overstuffed chair. She was crying, and Brian Riordan was beside her, patting her arm.

"What's all this?" Martin said.

"She learned that her husband took a powder, I think," the patrolman said.

Martin removed his hat and smoothed down his thin hair. Prior and Sheila sat down inconspicuously on a sofa while Jake lit a cigarette and walked to the fireplace where a small wood fire was burning. He turned his back to the heat gratefully.

Martin looked down at Denise.

"We've got a few things to clear up, Mrs. Riordan. I'll try to be as quick as possible."

Denise continued to cry and despite the solemnity of the scene the thought occurred to Jake that she would get a great deal of sympathy during Riordan's trial. She was wearing a black dress with sequins and the firelight played interestingly over her smooth tanned legs and gracefully molded ankles. Denise, Jake guessed, would do all right.

Brian Riordan said to Martin, "This is a helluva time to be barging in. Can't it wait until tomorrow?"

"No, it can't wait until tomorrow," Martin said.

"Okay, let's get it over with then," Brian said coldly.

A loud peremptory knock sounded and every head turned sharply. Martin stepped over and opened the door.

Gary Noble and Toni stood in the corridor.

"Come in," Martin said.

Martin closed the door behind them, and Noble glanced around the room uncertainly. "What the devil is going on?" he said. "Toni called me and said Niccolo was in some kind of trouble. What the hell is going on? Where's Riordan?"

"Dean Niccolo was murdered this evening," Martin said. "Dan Riordan has blown out of town. Is all this news to you, Mr. Noble?"

"Good God," Noble said.

Toni Ryerson turned frantically to Jake, and when he looked away from her, she took a backward step. "I knew he was in trouble, but I didn't know he was dead," she said. "It didn't matter that he was in trouble. I thought . . ."

She stopped speaking and sat down carefully in a straight-backed chair.

Noble patted her shoulder and said to Martin, "This is terrible."

"Yes, it is," Martin said.

Everyone was watching him expectantly now. He stood in the middle of the room, his eyes touching everyone present in turn and the silence became a heavy, palpable thing.

"All right," Brian said savagely. "What are we waiting for?"

Martin glanced at him calmly and then walked over and sat down beside Prior.

"Jake has something to tell us," he said, in a conversational voice. "I think you'll find it interesting."

Brian made an impatient gesture with his hand. "What the hell has he got to do with this matter?"

"Go ahead, Jake," Martin said.

Jake faced the semi-circle of puzzled faces with what he hoped was a confident expression, and tried to escape the feeling that he was as out of place as a thumb screw in a psychiatrist's office.

"I'm going to talk about three murders," he said. "The heart of this matter is, or was, May Laval, a gay and exciting woman whom we all knew. May made the mistake of deciding to publish her memoirs, the details of which were embarrassing and distressing to a number of important people. This is not the time to examine her motives for doing this, because the real reasons will probably never be known. Anyway, she

225

started her project, and was immediately marked to die."

He lit a cigarette and wished he hadn't ended the sentence so inanely. He was getting warmed up to his topic, but he would have preferred to write it down instead of delivering it like an earnest valedictorian. That was the trouble with murder, he decided irrelevantly. It was so damn obvious and blunt. You couldn't be casual about it. The minute you tried you sounded fatuous. All you could do was treat it seriously; and that made you appear pompous and slightly ridiculous. He sighed and blew a streamer of smoke into the air.

"One gentleman who didn't want his wartime activities put on the best-seller lists was Dan Riordan. He therefore sent his dog robber, Avery Meed, to cajole May out of writing a book. Riordan's offer consisted of straight, beautiful cash. But, and this is important, when Meed arrived at May Laval's home, May was already dead. She had been strangled before he got there.

"Meed may have been shocked by this fact, but he was well-trained enough to go on with his orders. He found the diary and took it to his hotel room.

"Now," Jake continued, "we come to an unlikely development. I mean Dean Niccolo. The pitch was consistent with Dean's behavior pattern, I suppose. And, parenthetically, everyone in this mess behaved with deplorable unoriginality. Everybody followed his characteristic bent religiously. Had anyone crossed us up by seeking peace of mind, or knowledge, or the love of a pure woman, we'd have been lost. But everybody behaved predictably, everybody wanted something for nothing.

"So, to get back to Dean Niccolo. He had been gambling. He got seriously into debt, and needed funds in a hurry. He knew that May Laval had some dirt on Riordan, so he decided to try to get hold of it, the object of course being blackmail. Therefore he went to May's home, arriving there just as Avery Meed was making his entrance. He watched Meed go inside and come out half a minute later with a book under his arm.

"Niccolo lost his nerve. He left. But the same morning he met Meed in my office, and learned that he worked for Riordan. Niccolo knew then from the papers that May had been killed and her diary stolen, so he guessed that Meed had done both jobs. He trailed Meed from our office to his apartment and made a proposition. But Meed was constitutionally unable to rebel against his orders and so he refused Niccolo's offer. That is why he died. Niccolo killed him and got hold of the diary.

"Now," Jake said, "we come to the end of act one. Is everyone following me so far?"

"How much more of this do we have to listen to?"

Brian asked Martin.

"Just until he's through," Martin said.

"I'm going to get more interesting from now on," Jake said, with a glance at Brian. "But let's not leave Niccolo quite so abruptly. One thing ruined his plan. Prior here had already discovered Riordan's wartime frauds—the frauds revealed in the diary. Thus, Prior knocked Niccolo out of a sale. Riordan wasn't interested in suppressing information at a fat figure, when the same dope was already in the Government's hands. Thus when Niccolo called Riordan to make a sale he was told to go to hell. Riordan knew Prior had the dope on him because Prior had told me and I, in turn, had told Riordan.

"That's enough background, I think. It's time to be vulgar and start pointing."

Jake put out his cigarette and lit another. He glanced around the room, and said, "Here's the way it could have happened, of course, with names and everything."

He turned to Brian and Denise.

"How long has your affair been going on?"

Denise said, "That's a fine thing to say."

"I know," Jake said. "But it's important to my theory." He glanced at Brian. "Do you have something melodramatic to say, or would you prefer to answer the question?"

Brian said coolly, "You're getting in nice and deep,

my friend. Go ahead."

"Why, thanks. Your father knew about the affair you'd been having with Denise, of course. Denise, who is majestically indiscreet when tight, let your father in on your secret."

"That's a lie," Denise said.

Jake smiled. "Hardly. Remember the afternoon you and I had a few drinks? We came back here and Riordan entered a few moments later. You were lying on the couch and, to be a heel about it, you were stinking drunk. He told you to get to your room, whereupon you began to entreat him to take you up to the lodge again—a place you'd never been with Riordan. You said as much the first night I met you in Noble's office. Riordan then learned that you had been up to the lodge, and that you were well aware of its aphrodisiac qualities—or the aphrodisiac qualities of its usual tenant. Riordan reasoned thus: you'd been to the lodge, ergo, it must have been with Brian."

"I won't listen to any more of this," Brian shouted.

"When your father realized that you were two-timing him with his wife, he kicked you out," Jake said calmly. "He'd taken quite a beating from you, Brian. He listened to your cynical moralizing about the war, and watched you posturing absurdly as the bitter, maladjusted war hero. Why he did is something a psychiatrist might tell us. But he drew the line at allowing you to play around with Denise."

Brian shrugged and lit a cigarette. "You're being awfully wordy about it. We had a disagreement and he blew his top, that's all."

"There's a little more to it than that. What did you do when you realized that the golden eggs weren't going to be laid any more?"

"Oh, that's your story," Brian said with a smile.

"Okay. When you were tossed out of your mink-lined nest you started thinking how you could clip him for some money." Jake stopped and turned casually to Denise. "Remember, Denise, when you told me about your habit of listening in on the extension phone in your bedroom?"

Denise glanced uncertainly at Brian, and then said, "I may have mentioned it. It's hardly a crime."

"Well, that depends. Dean Niccolo made a call from here this afternoon. He called a girl named Toni Ryerson who is sitting with us now. Did that conversation surprise you?"

"Don't say anything!" Brian said. "That's none of his damned business."

"Yes, you'd better be extremely careful now," Jake said. "Dean called Toni to ask her to help him out of an embarrassing spot. Dean talked too much to me—he mentioned knowing that I'd received May's diary—and he had to have an alibi. You see he had sent me the diary, after killing Meed. The police could have used that information, Denise. Why didn't you go to them?"

"I didn't know what the devil he was talking about," Denise said, standing and facing him excitedly. "It didn't make any sense to me."

"Shut up," Brian said.

"Damn it," Denise said, wheeling on him. "I'm tired of being shouted at. I couldn't make any sense out of it, and neither could you."

Jake said, "So you told Brian about the call, eh? And Brian was confused and bewildered?"

"She told me about a conversation she'd overheard between Niccolo and some girl," Brian said tensely. "Do what you can with that."

"I'm going to try. You knew from that conversation that Niccolo had sent me the diary. That meant that Niccolo had clipped the stuff pertaining to your father from the diary and still had it in his possession —since I told your father, in your presence remember, that the diary received had no reference to him in it. You knew that Niccolo had the dirt on your father. And you wanted a way to make your father start laying those golden eggs again, didn't you? So you thought of blackmail."

Brian pushed a lock of hair from his forehead and attempted a smile. It was not a success.

He said, "Supposing you say what you mean in simple blunt language."

"Fine," Jake said. "I'm suggesting that you might have gone to Niccolo's tonight, after learning he had the dirt on your father, and that you blew his brains out when he wouldn't come across with the clipping. Didn't you?"

Brian shook his head. "No," he said.

Lieutenant Martin got up slowly and rubbed the back of his head with his left hand. "You took a drive out toward Niccolo's apartment tonight, didn't you?" he said, in a mild voice.

Brian turned to him with a startled expression. "You're not taking this pipe dream seriously, are you?"

"Oh, very seriously," Lieutenant Martin said.

"You can't be," Brian cried. "You're trying to pin this on me to frame me, that's all."

Denise had been watching him tensely since Martin had spoken; and now she suddenly took a step back and put a hand to her mouth. "You killed him," she whispered. "You simple fool. I told you . . ."

Brian turned and slapped her across the mouth with his open hand.

"You simply won't keep quiet, will you?" he said coolly.

"That's enough of the dramatics," Martin said. He looked at Jake thoughtfully for a second, a worried line above his eyes; then he shrugged. "Okay," he said to Brian. "Let's go."

The words seemed to act as a spur to Brian. He

lunged forward suddenly and hurled Martin aside, and then broke for the door.

But he didn't get far. Prior came out of his chair with astonishing speed, caught him by the shoulder and spun him round; and before Brian regained his balance, Prior straightened him with a savage right to the jaw. Brian's eyes glazed over as he started to fall; and Prior's next punch, a professionally expert left hook, dropped him to the floor unconscious.

A uniformed policeman stepped quickly over his prostrate body and caught Denise by the arms as she started for the door.

"That was neat work," Martin said to Prior. He brushed his hair down. "He caught me by surprise."

"Well, you were busy talking, and I had a better chance to watch," Prior said. "I saw it coming."

Sheila slipped over to Jake. "You were wonderful," she said. "Now can we get out of here?"

"Oh, sure," Jake said, and looked at Martin who was scratching his ear and frowning somberly. "We'll clear out right away. But first we've got to settle something."

He paused and glanced around the room.

"You see, Brian didn't murder Niccolo. The emotional difficulties in the Riordan family had nothing to do with that murder—or May's.

"The fact that Denise overheard a conversation, that Dan Riordan absconded, and that Brian and

Denise enjoyed an affair had nothing to do with Niccolo's murder—or May's. But they all formed so neat and logical a pattern that I was seduced. The person who murdered May and Niccolo was quite obvious for some time. I outlined a case against Brian and Denise just to show you all how misleading those developments were. And of course I had to show off a little too."

"Well," Martin demanded.

"Oh, yes," Jake said. He turned and glanced at another person in the room. "How about it, Prior? Shall I tell the story, or will you?"

Prior started. He stared at Jake for several seconds and then smoothed his closely cropped hair with an absent gesture and smiled slightly. "Now what the hell do you mean by that, Jake?"

"I mean that you murdered May Laval and Dean Niccolo," Jake said, easily. "Would you like to hear the details?"

Prior lit a cigarette and smiled again, and then he said, "Well, I guess you'd better explain yourself," in a puzzled but unworried voice.

CHAPTER FIFTEEN

Prior lit the cigarette he had in his mouth and dropped the lighter into his vest pocket. "Jake, I hope you know what you're doing," he said.

"Don't worry," Jake said. "I know precisely what I'm doing. You murdered May because you feared the details of your long-ago affair with her might become public knowledge."

He smiled without humor as color mounted suddenly in Prior's face.

"Offhand," Jake said, "I can't think of a more embarrassing development in the career of a shining knight from the Hampstead Committee."

Prior stared at Jake unseeingly and then put a hand to his forehead and sat down stiffly, like someone who had received without a warning a piece of shocking news. For an instant he seemed oblivious to everyone and everything in the room. And then he took his hand down and his features were hard, wary, appraising.

Jake glanced at Martin who nodded with finality.

"Yes," Jake said. "That does it, I think."

"But go on," Martin said. "I'd like to hear it all."

"Okay," Jake said, and lit a cigarette. He sat on the arm of an overstuffed chair, and took Sheila's hand. She squeezed his fingers with quick, intimate pressure, and he smiled at her before glancing back to Martin.

"The big thing of course was this: Prior came to me and said he had evidence of Riordan's wartime peculations—evidence he claimed to have gotten from the Riordan Company's official books and records. Prior had the details, including the name of the man who okayed the faulty barrels, Nickerson. I'm not certain why Prior did this, but my guess is he hoped to convince me there was no point in defending Riordan. You see, in the first exchange, we had made Prior look very bad, so bad, in fact, that Senator Hampstead had flown in and raised hell with him. Prior wanted to prevent that from happening again; and he thought it would slow me down to know that their case against Riordan was unassailable.

"But getting back to the main point: Prior's information surprised me. Avery Meed had previously told me that the Riordan Company books were doctored by experts to hide what was going on. And yet Prior hadn't been sidetracked or fooled. My first thought was that Meed had overestimated the astuteness of his accountants.

"Later that day I told Riordan what I'd learned from Prior. Riordan, of course, must have known instantly that Prior was on the right track; but Riordan didn't tell me that. He did say, parenthetically, that Nickerson, the government inspector, had died. I imagine Riordan made up his mind then to convert as much of his holdings as he could into cash and clear out. He had just learned that his wife was untrue, and my information told him that Prior would soon be breathing down his neck. And so I'm sure he started planning right then to get out."

Martin said, "It's a good guess."

"But it's not important," Jake said, "except as an interesting sidelight on life in America. The important thing was that I decided to pass on to Prior the news that Nickerson had died. I didn't get hold of Prior—he was leaving the office with Hampstead when I arrived—but I talked to his assistant, Gil Coombs, who is an accountant in charge of digging through the Riordan records.

"But Coombs knew nothing of Prior's information. The name Nickerson—supposedly gleaned from the Riordan Company records—meant absolutely nothing to him. He had to write it down on a piece of paper to make sure he wouldn't forget it.

"The significance of that escaped me at the time. But it eventually dawned. Prior couldn't have gotten his information from the Riordan Company records.

If he had, Coombs would have known, too.

"Therefore Prior had lied. Secondly, I started to wonder where he had gotten his information. And that wasn't too difficult to guess. May Laval's diary, of course. Prior also lied about another thing. He said he didn't know Chicago, but as Coombs told me he knew it well enough to act as a guide to its remotest joy spots."

Jake put out his cigarette, glanced at Prior and then back to Martin. "You can see what that meant? Prior knew May well enough to look through her diary, or else he'd seen it at some time when she wasn't around. Yet he had said he had never known or heard of May—obviously a flat lie.

"Now there were two questions to answer: One, when had he seen May's diary; and two, where had he seen it? I started with the where. Well, undoubtedly, in May's home. That's where the diary was until Avery Meed got hold of it. It was unlikely that Prior had seen it after Meed got it, because Meed took it home and it was still there when Niccolo killed him. Niccolo had it until he mailed it to me, and the stuff he clipped from it that pertained to Riordan was in his apartment—so, there was just no way for Prior to have seen it after Meed got it. Therefore he saw the diary in May's apartment some time before Meed arrived.

"That brought me to the when. Well, there was a

Mr. X at May's home early that morning. Gary Noble got there at two o'clock and she told him she was expecting a visitor at three. Now that visitor was gone when Meed arrived—and when Meed arrived May was dead."

Martin said, "And you decided that Prior was Mr. X?"

"It was inevitable," Jake said. "It was just a question of arithmetic. Also, Prior had made one more damaging slip. Talking to me he mentioned May's red pajamas—an item he couldn't have known about unless he'd been in her home that morning, at the time she was wearing the red Mandarin pajamas. I happen to remember she was wearing the red pajamas because Noble told me she was—but Prior's knowledge had to, and did, come at first hand. He had been to her home; he had seen the diary some time between three and four, when Meed arrived and found May was dead. That's when he saw May in the red Mandarin pajamas."

"That's why you borrowed Murphy, eh?" Martin said.

"Of course. The minute I saw the clips from the diary I knew I was right. There, in May's handwriting, was the same story Prior had told, with Nickerson's name and all the rest of it.

"And I also knew then that Prior had murdered Niccolo. Prior probably realized he'd made a mistake

239

in telling me what he'd learned from May's diary. Any minute I might wake up and ask myself: *How did he know?* It was imperative that he get the clips from the diary and destroy them. But he didn't know where they were. Then Niccolo called him tonight with the hope of selling him the information. Prior told him to go to hell—and then got out there as fast as he could to get the clips and also put Niccolo out of the way. He shot Niccolo and started a search for the clips. And got scared off by the prospect of someone finding him on the scene."

Jake lit another cigarette and blew out a stream of gray-blue smoke. The patrolman had released Denise and she was rubbing her arms and watching Jake closely. Brian still lay on the floor. Noble looked as if he wanted desperately to speak, but couldn't think of an opening wedge.

"It occurred to me then," Jake said, "that the whole story would have to come from May. I began to wonder if there might be another diary—one covering the last day or so of her life. And of course there was. Not a diary, but a dictaphone recording."

He looked at Prior. "You forgot about that, didn't you?"

Prior spread his hands and looked at them expressionlessly and then he sighed and rubbed his forehead with the tips of his fingers. "It doesn't matter," he said thickly.

Jake watched the irrelevant patterns made by the smoke curling from his cigarette. "I heard May's story tonight," he said. "The story was about Prior. How May met him in 1944 when he was a clerk for the War Resources Board. She reminisced about their brief and not too exciting affair, and discussed with considerable humor the fact that even then he had considered her a social liability. He couldn't be seen with her, and he couldn't introduce her to his friends. May was amused because she delighted in making him feel that he was degrading himself.

"Then Prior swam back into May's ken, and she was doubly amused, because he'd heard about the book she was going to write, and he was terrified that she would include him in the cast. Prior knew that Senator Hampstead's reaction would be volcanic if his chief investigator turned up in a Sunday supplement role in an exposé of wartime fornication and chicanery. Hampstead would plant his foot squarely in Prior's posterior and kick him right out of Washington.

"So Prior begged May not to use anything about him. And she agreed. But Prior wasn't satisfied. He asked to see the diary, to make sure he wasn't in it, and May said all right. And he had another request. Would May call his assistant, Coombs, and make an appointment with them for the next morning? Prior needed an excuse for knowing May—he knew he'd meet her—and if she made the first overture that would explain his knowing her.

"Well, Prior saw the diary. And he wasn't in it. And then he realized that that wasn't enough. If May was going to be involved in the Riordan investigation —as she would have been—their previous relationship would be smoked out. Reporters would have gotten hold of it, and Riordan's lawyers and press agents would find out about it and use it for all it was worth to discredit Prior. He probably saw himself humiliated, excoriated, and broken because of the scandal.

"That is guesswork of course. I don't know what the hell he was thinking about. But the fact is he put a sash around her throat and strangled her. Who can say why he did it? One person murders another and later on it is decided it was a crime of passion, of revenge, or lust, or a hundred other things, but the real reason exists probably for one split second while the murder is committed and after that the motivations become blurred and meaningless."

Jake smiled tiredly. "This recondite philosophizing is tossed in without charge. Getting back to the raw facts, however, Prior, in looking at May's diary, saw the dope on Riordan, and being efficient, made a note of it for use in his work. That, in the classic parlance, was his first and fatal mistake."

He glanced to Martin. "That's the works. It's all

yours now."

Martin cleared his throat and walked over to Prior and put a hand on his shoulder. "You'd better get ready," he said. "I'm taking you in."

Prior was still rubbing his forehead. "All right," he said in a low voice.

There was a knock at the door and Murphy came in, a portable Dictaphone under his arm. He made a circle of his thumb and forefinger and smiled at Jake. "Right on the dot."

"I don't think we'll need it," Martin said.

Murphy took an object wrapped in a handkerchief from his pocket and said, "This is for you, Lieutenant. Davis sent it over. He said you were right."

Martin unwrapped the handkerchief carefully and displayed a nickel-plated .32 revolver. He smiled at Jake. "I knew that Prior and May were close friends for a month or so back in '43. We got that the way we get damn near everything in police work, by scrounging and hunting around and asking a thousand questions. So when Prior lied about knowing her I got interested and put a tail on him. Prior went out toward Niccolo's apartment tonight but my man lost him. I told him to get over to Prior's hotel, too, and take a look around. This is what he found. It's probably the gun that killed Niccolo."

Jake took Sheila's arm and said to Martin, "You don't need me any more, I'm sure."

"Just one thing. What about those lipsticked crosses on the mirror, and so forth?"

Jake said, "Prior did that, I would guess, in an attempt to disguise the reason for her murder. He made it look like a Black Hand killing as a pulp writer would imagine it. It should have been an immediate tip-off, you know."

"What do you mean?"

"Well, it was corny, unimaginative and routine. If we had looked for someone like that we'd have found Prior."

"Yeah?" Martin said dubiously, and then pushed Jake lightly on the shoulder. "Thanks, friend. If you need a job come see me."

Jake grabbed Sheila and started for the door, but Brian Riordan, who had gotten to his feet, stepped in front of him.

"Wait a minute, smart man," he said. "What was the idea of teeing off on me and Denise?"

Jake studied him calmly and then glanced at Denise who had come to Brian's side.

"I kind of thought you deserved it," he said mildly. "You're a delightful pair of people, you know."

Denise flushed but Brian forced a mocking smile to his lips. "What have you got to be so damned superior about?" he said.

"Didn't you know?" Jake smiled. "I'm a noble character. I quit my job because it involved meeting too many people like you. Now if you'll excuse me."

He opened the door and put his arm about Sheila's waist as they walked briskly toward the elevators. "Darling, you were superb!" Sheila said. "I was so damn proud of you."

"Naturally," Jake grinned.

A shout from behind caused them to stop; and when they turned they saw Noble hurrying toward them along the corridor, an anxious, pleading expression on his face.

"Jake, old man," he said. "You can't run out like this. I need you."

"That's unfortunate," Jake said.

Noble looked as if he might weep. "Jake, you've just got a mild attack of morals. It'll pass over in a day or so. Come in and see me, eh? There'll be other accounts like Riordan, don't forget."

Jake patted Noble on the shoulder. "Thanks for reminding me of that, Gary. When my resolution falters I'll hold that thought before me and take strength from it."

The elevator door slid open and Jake stepped inside with Sheila.

"Remember me to the mob," he said, as the door slid shut in Noble's stricken face.

As they came through the revolving doors the doorman smiled politely at them and went into the street and began blowing his whistle.

Jake and Sheila stood close together watching the snow that fell like a dotted Swiss curtain between them and the cold night. The only sound was the cheery piping of the doorman's whistle.

Sheila turned suddenly and put her hands on his shoulders. There were a few snowflakes in her hair and her eyes were shining. "Let's go home," she said, "to my apartment. I still make wonderful breakfasts. Is that all right?"

Jake kissed her and said, "It's the best offer I've had today."

The doorman thanked Jake for the bill he put in his hand; and then he looked at it again, and said, "*Thank* you, sir," and closed the cab door behind them reverently.

They drove out Michigan Boulevard and Sheila snuggled close to him.

Something occurred to Jake then and he put his hand carefully into his breast pocket and removed Mike Francesca's card. He looked at it with a slight smile. Mike wanted a public relations man and would probably be a liberal boss.

He glanced down at Sheila and after a moment or so sighed philosophically and dropped Mike's card out the window.

Sheila stirred and said, "What was that?"

Jake kissed the top of her head. "Just the dear dead past," he said.

THE END

For a complete list of books available from Penguin in the United States, write to Dept. DG, Penguin Books, 299 Murray Hill Parkway, East Rutherford, New Jersey 07073.